# PEANUTS EVERY SUNDAY

WUMP

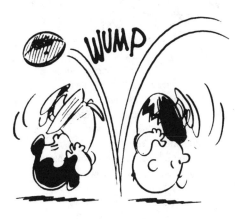

# PEANUTS CLASSICS

*Dr. Beagle and Mr. Hyde*
*Fly, You Stupid Kite, Fly!*
*How Long, Great Pumpkin, How Long?*
*It's Great to Be a Superstar*
*Kiss Her, You Blockhead!*
*My Anxieties Have Anxieties*
*Speak Softly, and Carry a Beagle*
*There Goes the Shutout*
*Summers Fly, Winters Walk*
*Thank Goodness for People*
*The Beagle Has Landed*
*What Makes You Think You're Happy?*
*And a Woodstock in a Birch Tree*
*A Smile Makes a Lousy Umbrella*
*The Mad Punter Strikes Again*
*There's a Vulture Outside*
*Here Comes the April Fool!*
*What Makes Musicians So Sarcastic?*
*A Kiss on the Nose Turns Anger Aside*
*It's Hard Work Being Bitter*
*I'm Not Your Sweet Babboo!*
*Stop Snowing on My Secretary*
*Always Stick Up for the Underbird*
*What's Wrong with Being Crabby?*
*Don't Hassle Me with Your Sighs, Chuck*
*The Way of the Fussbudget Is Not Easy*
*You're Weird, Sir!*
*It's a Long Way to Tipperary*
*Who's the Funny-Looking Kid with the Big Nose?*
*Sunday's Fun Day, Charlie Brown*
*You're Out of Your Mind, Charlie Brown!*
*You're the Guest of Honor, Charlie Brown*
*You Can't Win, Charlie Brown*
*Peanuts Every Sunday*
*The Unsinkable Charlie Brown*
*Good Grief, More Peanuts*

# PEANUTS EVERY SUNDAY

## by Charles M. Schulz

An Owl Book
Henry Holt and Company/ New York

Henry Holt and Company, Inc.
*Publishers since 1866*
115 West 18th Street
New York, New York 10011

Henry Holt® is a registered trademark
of Henry Holt and Company, Inc.

Published in Canada by Fitzhenry & Whiteside Ltd.,
195 Allstate Parkway, Markham, Ontario L3R 4T8.

Library of Congress Catalog Card Number: 94-76080

ISBN 0-8050-3310-6 (An Owl Book: pbk.)

Henry Holt books are available for special promotions
and premiums. For details contact: Director, Special Markets

Originally published as *Peanuts Every Sunday* in 1961 by
Holt, Rinehart and Winston. Published by Holt, Rinehart and
Winston in two parts in two expanded editions under the
titles *What Makes Musicians So Sarcastic?* in 1976 and
*Thank Goodness for People* in 1976.

New Owl Book Edition—1994

Printed in the United States of America
All first editions are printed on acid-free paper.∞

1   3   5   7   9   10   8   6   4   2

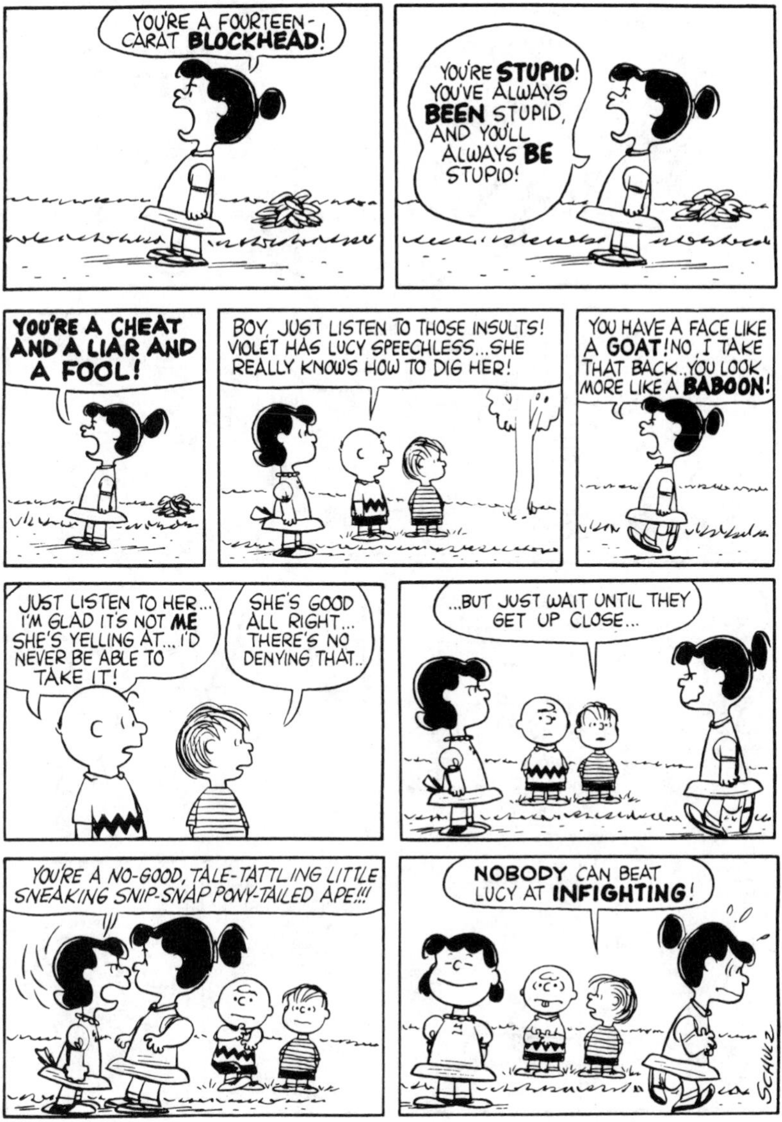

YOU'RE A FOURTEEN-CARAT **BLOCKHEAD**!
YOU'RE **STUPID**! YOU'VE ALWAYS **BEEN** STUPID, AND YOU'LL ALWAYS **BE** STUPID!
**YOU'RE A CHEAT AND A LIAR AND A FOOL!**
BOY, JUST LISTEN TO THOSE INSULTS! VIOLET HAS LUCY SPEECHLESS...SHE REALLY KNOWS HOW TO DIG HER!
YOU HAVE A FACE LIKE A **GOAT**! NO, I TAKE THAT BACK..YOU LOOK MORE LIKE A **BABOON**!
JUST LISTEN TO HER... I'M GLAD IT'S NOT **ME** SHE'S YELLING AT... I'D NEVER BE ABLE TO TAKE IT!
SHE'S GOOD ALL RIGHT... THERE'S NO DENYING THAT..
...BUT JUST WAIT UNTIL THEY GET UP CLOSE...
*YOU'RE A NO-GOOD, TALE-TATTLING LITTLE SNEAKING SNIP-SNAP PONY-TAILED APE!!!*
**NOBODY** CAN BEAT LUCY AT **INFIGHTING**!
SCHULZ

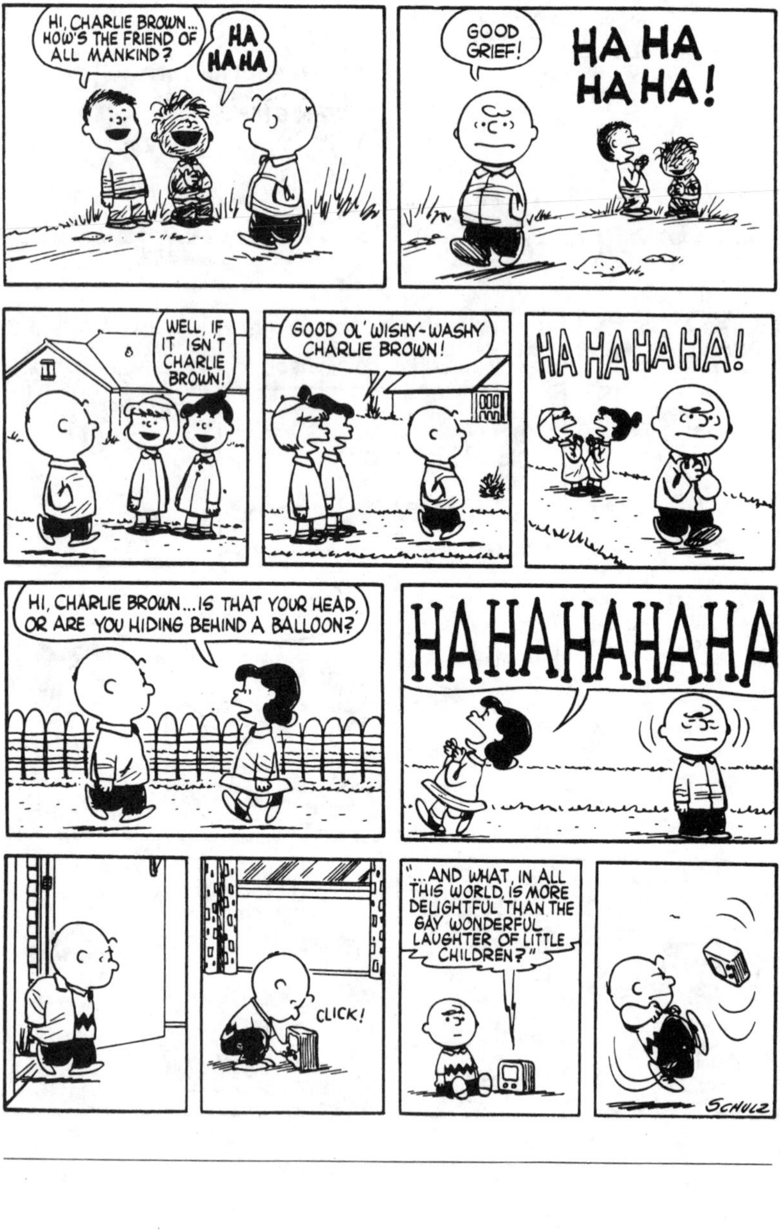

HI, CHARLIE BROWN... HOW'S THE FRIEND OF ALL MANKIND?
HA HA HA
GOOD GRIEF!
HA HA HA HA!
WELL, IF IT ISN'T CHARLIE BROWN!
GOOD OL' WISHY-WASHY CHARLIE BROWN!
HA HA HA HA HA!
HI, CHARLIE BROWN...IS THAT YOUR HEAD, OR ARE YOU HIDING BEHIND A BALLOON?
HAHAHAHAHAHA
CLICK!
"...AND WHAT, IN ALL THIS WORLD, IS MORE DELIGHTFUL THAN THE GAY WONDERFUL LAUGHTER OF LITTLE CHILDREN?"
SCHULZ

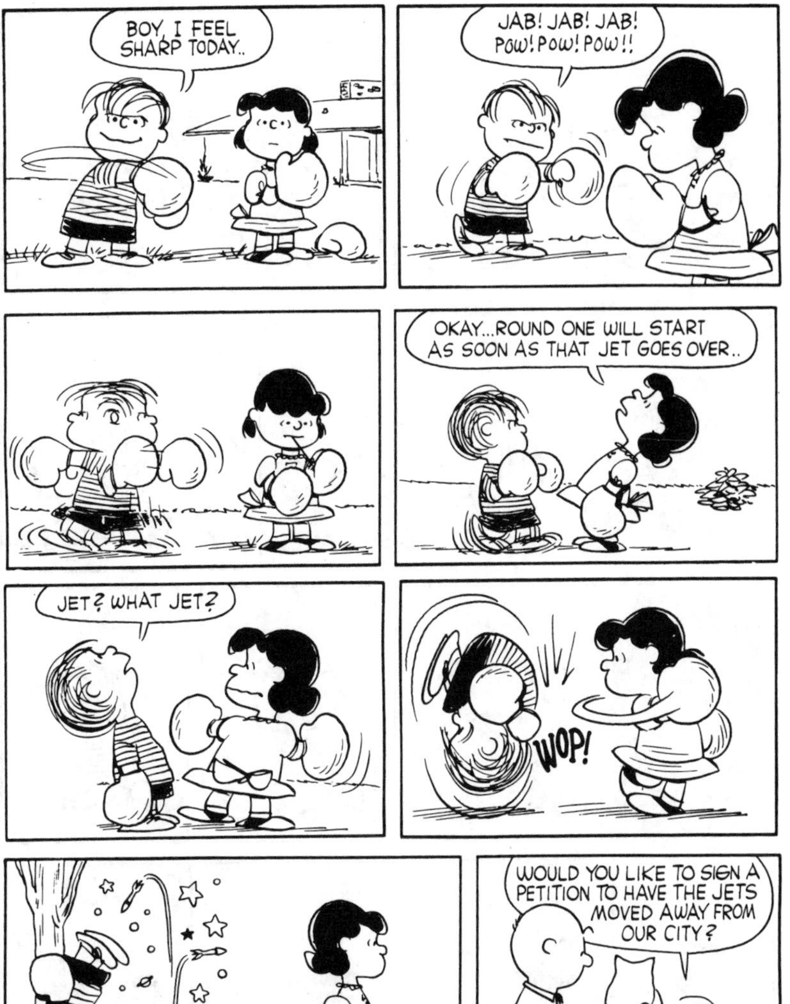
BOY, I FEEL SHARP TODAY..
JAB! JAB! JAB! POW! POW! POW!!
OKAY...ROUND ONE WILL START AS SOON AS THAT JET GOES OVER..
JET? WHAT JET?
WOP!
WOULD YOU LIKE TO SIGN A PETITION TO HAVE THE JETS MOVED AWAY FROM OUR CITY?

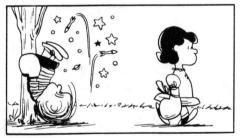

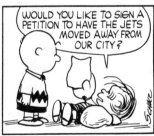

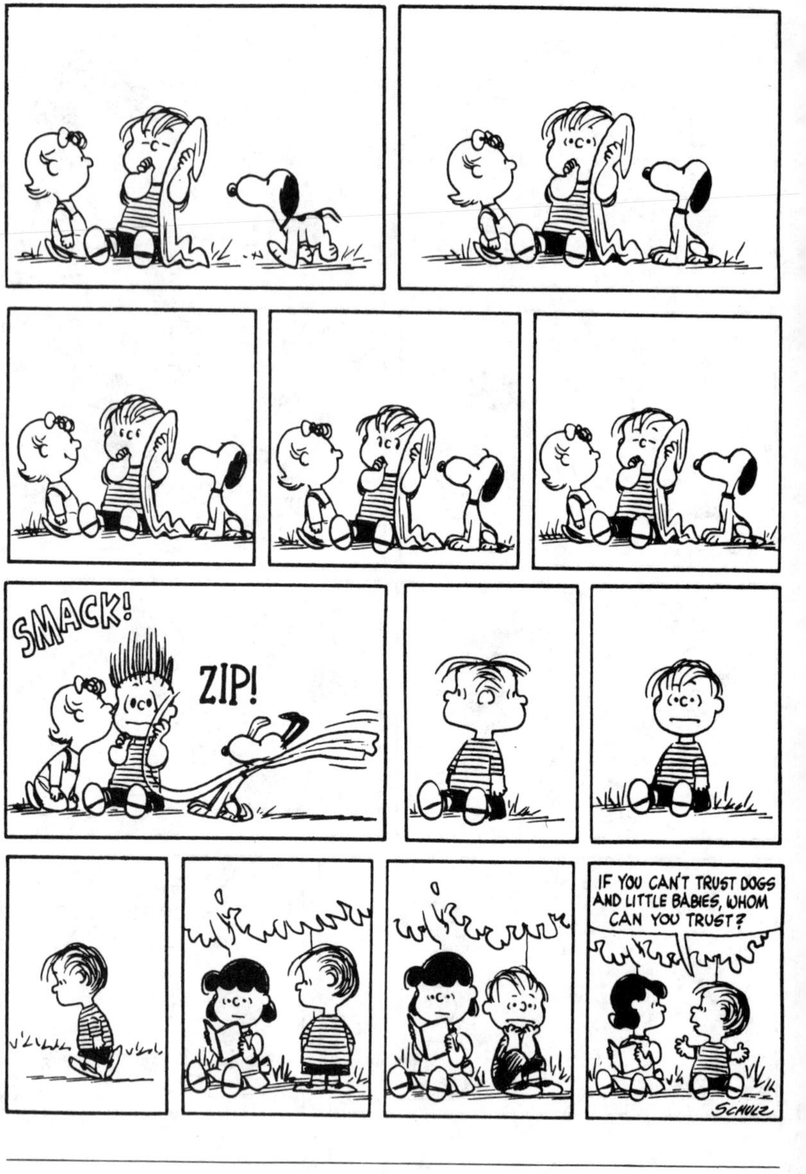
SMACK!
ZIP!
IF YOU CAN'T TRUST DOGS AND LITTLE BABIES, WHOM CAN YOU TRUST?
SCHULZ

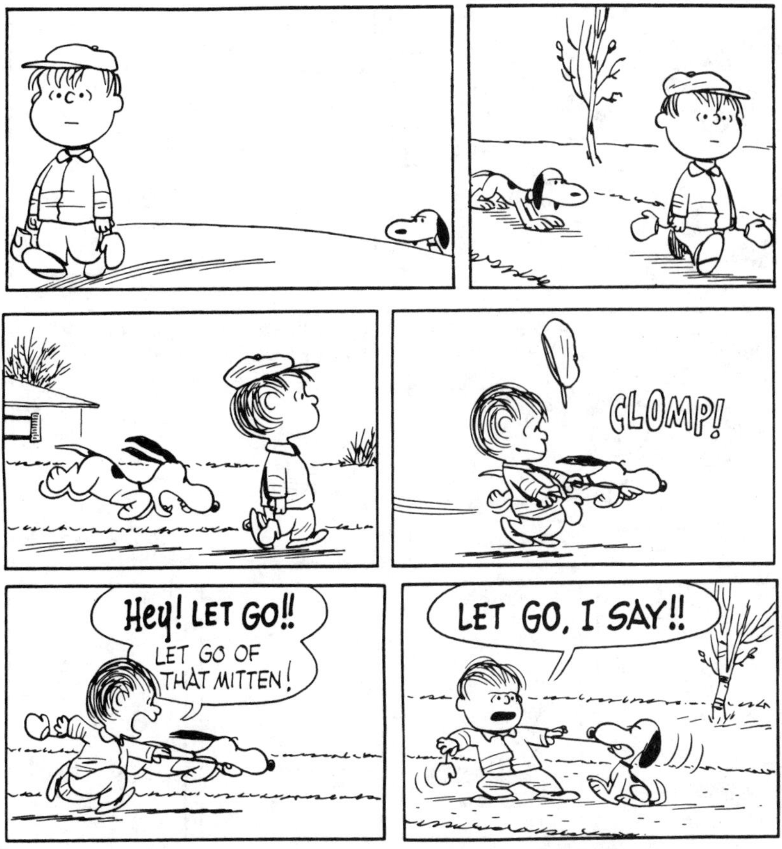
CLOMP!
Hey! LET GO!!
LET GO OF THAT MITTEN!
LET GO, I SAY!!
WOOP!
THEY SURE HAVE A LOT OF NEW THINGS THESE DAYS FOR DOGS TO WEAR IN COLD WEATHER..
SCHULZ

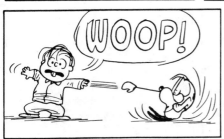

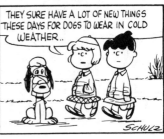

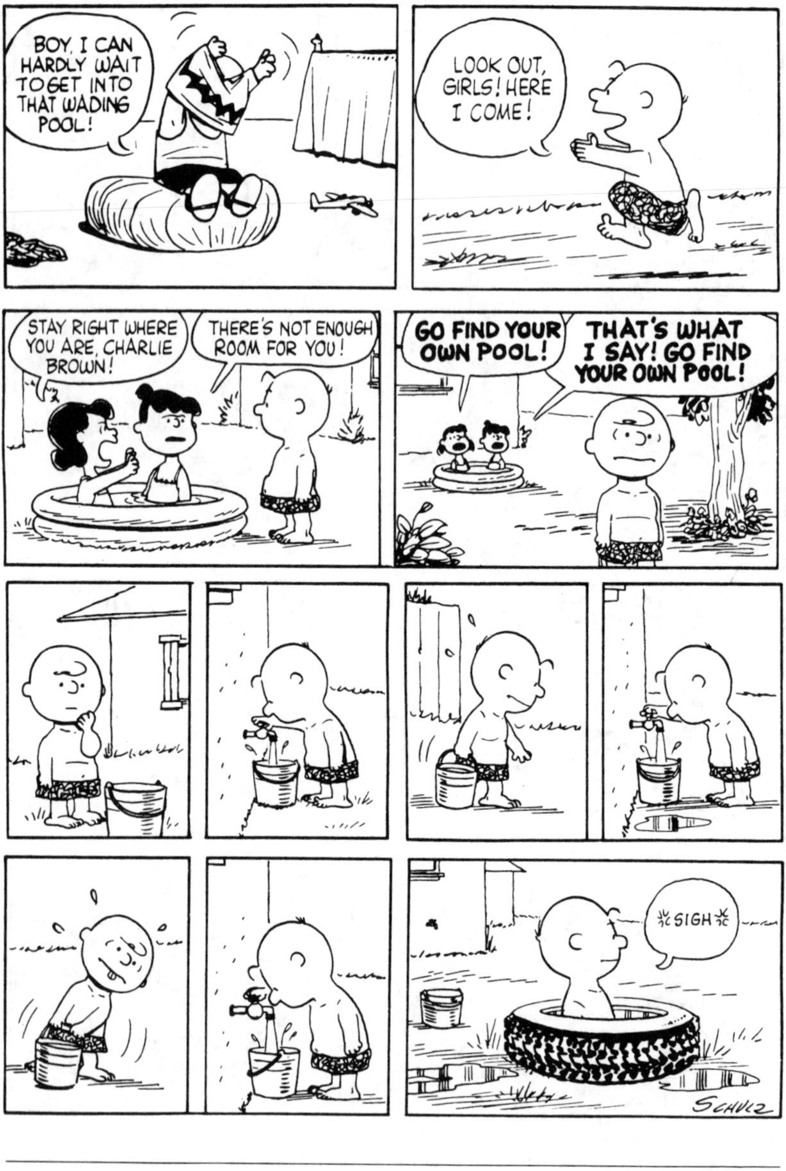
BOY, I CAN HARDLY WAIT TO GET INTO THAT WADING POOL!
LOOK OUT, GIRLS! HERE I COME!
STAY RIGHT WHERE YOU ARE, CHARLIE BROWN!
THERE'S NOT ENOUGH ROOM FOR YOU!
GO FIND YOUR OWN POOL!
THAT'S WHAT I SAY! GO FIND YOUR OWN POOL!
SIGH
SCHULZ

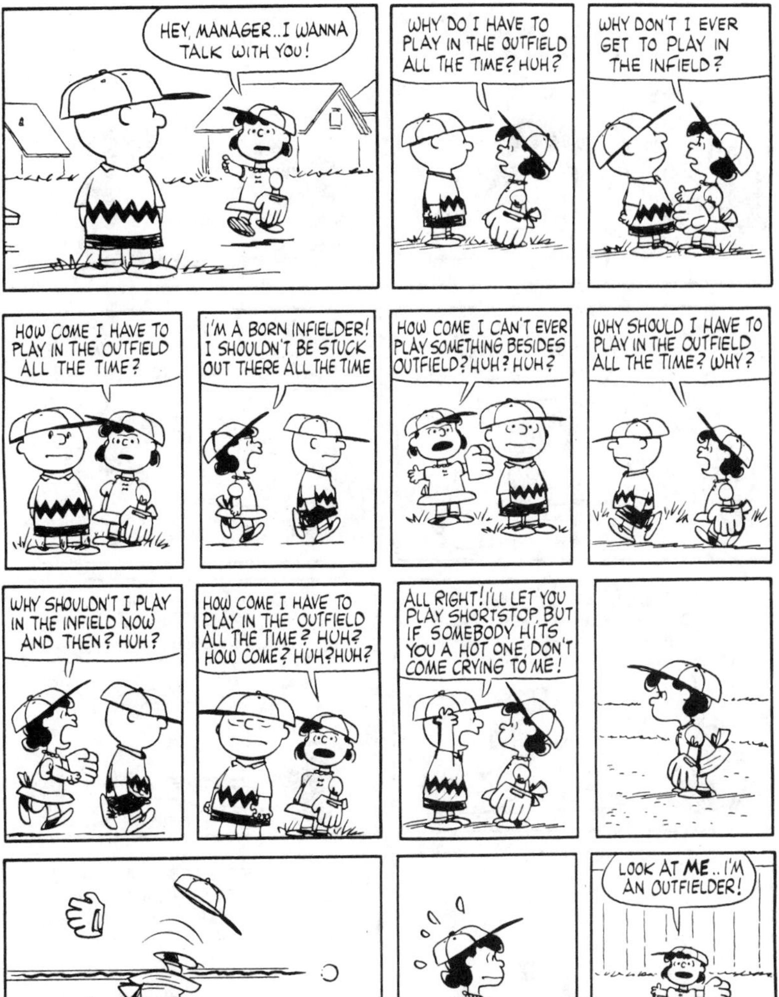

HEY, MANAGER..I WANNA TALK WITH YOU!
WHY DO I HAVE TO PLAY IN THE OUTFIELD ALL THE TIME? HUH?
WHY DON'T I EVER GET TO PLAY IN THE INFIELD?
HOW COME I HAVE TO PLAY IN THE OUTFIELD ALL THE TIME?
I'M A BORN INFIELDER! I SHOULDN'T BE STUCK OUT THERE ALL THE TIME
HOW COME I CAN'T EVER PLAY SOMETHING BESIDES OUTFIELD? HUH? HUH?
WHY SHOULD I HAVE TO PLAY IN THE OUTFIELD ALL THE TIME? WHY?
WHY SHOULDN'T I PLAY IN THE INFIELD NOW AND THEN? HUH?
HOW COME I HAVE TO PLAY IN THE OUTFIELD ALL THE TIME? HUH? HOW COME? HUH? HUH?
ALL RIGHT! I'LL LET YOU PLAY SHORTSTOP, BUT IF SOMEBODY HITS YOU A HOT ONE, DON'T COME CRYING TO ME!
POW!
LOOK AT ME.. I'M AN OUTFIELDER!
SCHULZ

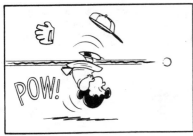

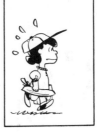

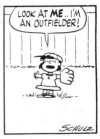

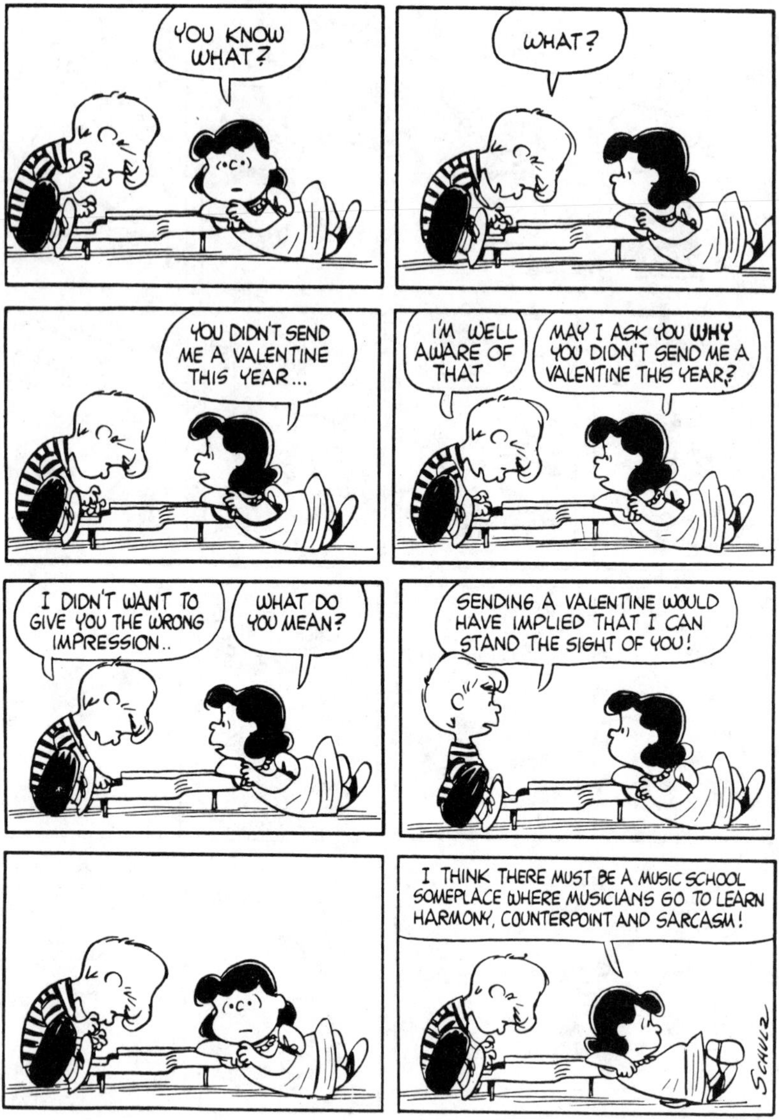
YOU KNOW WHAT?
WHAT?
YOU DIDN'T SEND ME A VALENTINE THIS YEAR...
I'M WELL AWARE OF THAT
MAY I ASK YOU WHY YOU DIDN'T SEND ME A VALENTINE THIS YEAR?
I DIDN'T WANT TO GIVE YOU THE WRONG IMPRESSION..
WHAT DO YOU MEAN?
SENDING A VALENTINE WOULD HAVE IMPLIED THAT I CAN STAND THE SIGHT OF YOU!
I THINK THERE MUST BE A MUSIC SCHOOL SOMEPLACE WHERE MUSICIANS GO TO LEARN HARMONY, COUNTERPOINT AND SARCASM!
SCHULZ

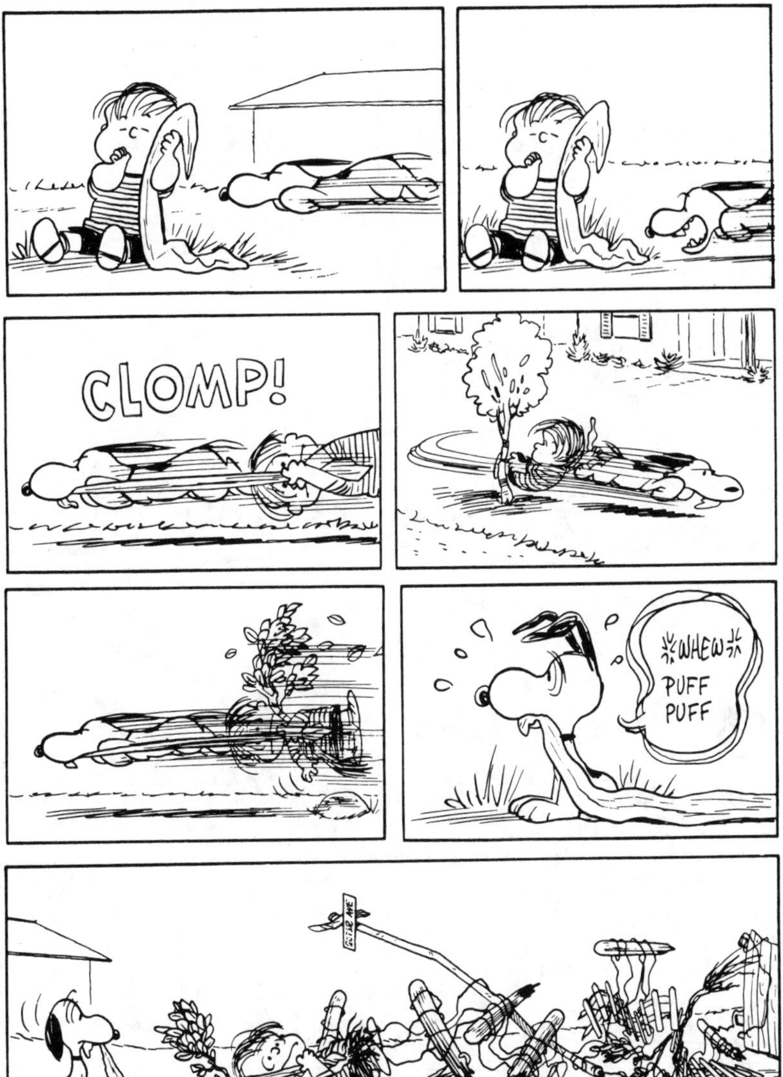
CLOMP!
WHEW
PUFF
PUFF

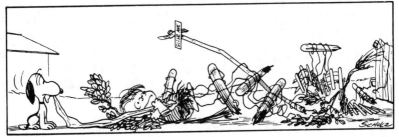

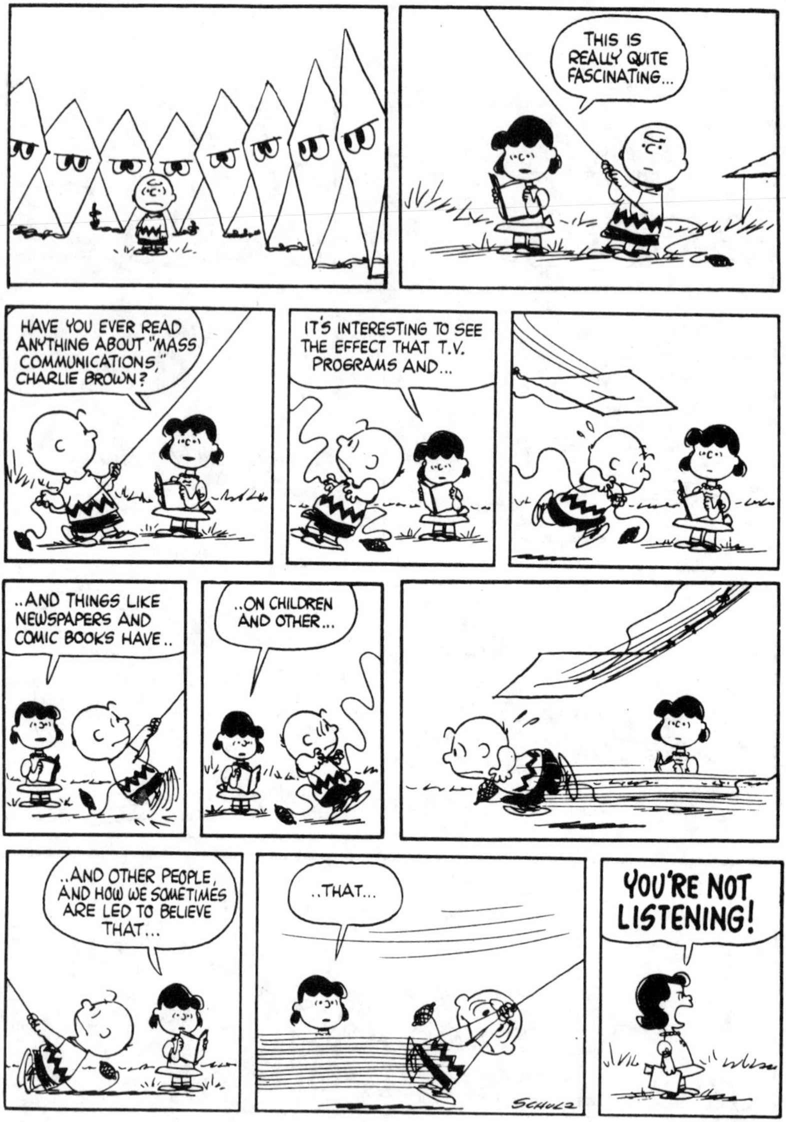
THIS IS REALLY QUITE FASCINATING...
HAVE YOU EVER READ ANYTHING ABOUT "MASS COMMUNICATIONS," CHARLIE BROWN?
IT'S INTERESTING TO SEE THE EFFECT THAT T.V. PROGRAMS AND...
..AND THINGS LIKE NEWSPAPERS AND COMIC BOOKS HAVE..
..ON CHILDREN AND OTHER...
..AND OTHER PEOPLE, AND HOW WE SOMETIMES ARE LED TO BELIEVE THAT...
..THAT...
YOU'RE NOT LISTENING!
SCHULZ

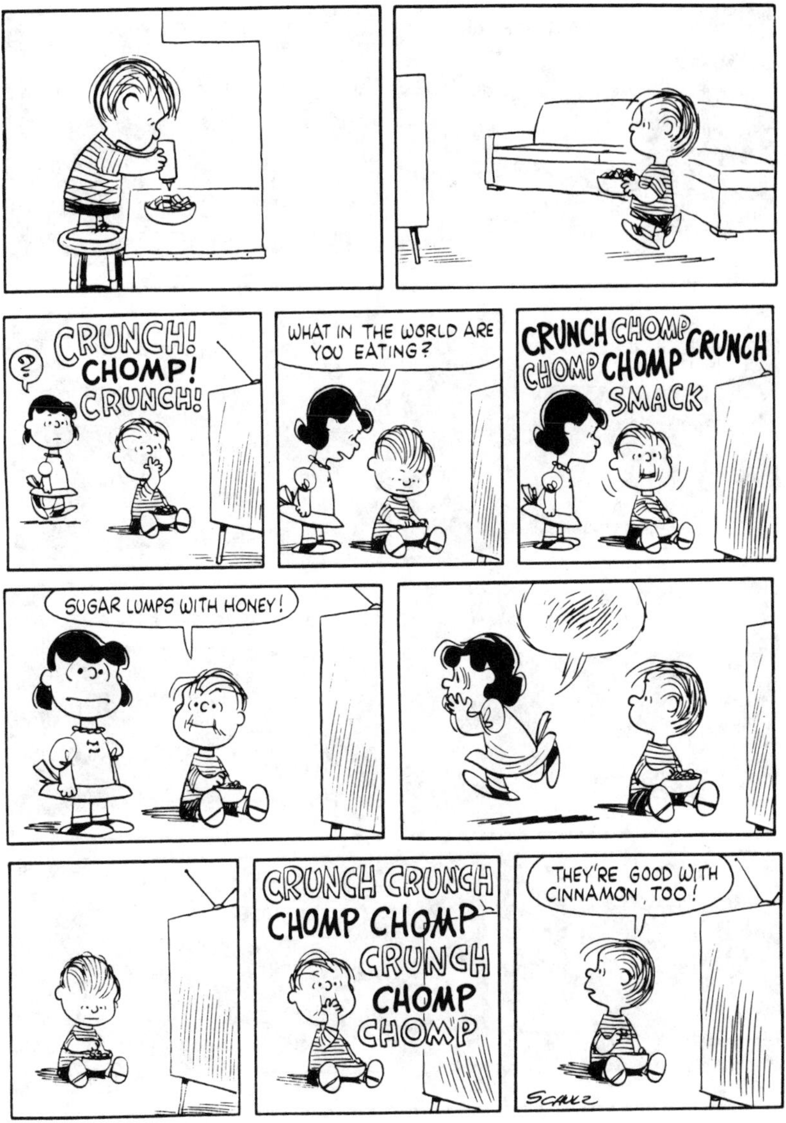

CRUNCH! CHOMP! CRUNCH!
?
WHAT IN THE WORLD ARE YOU EATING?
CRUNCH CHOMP CRUNCH CHOMP CHOMP SMACK
SUGAR LUMPS WITH HONEY!
CRUNCH CRUNCH CHOMP CHOMP CRUNCH CHOMP CHOMP
THEY'RE GOOD WITH CINNAMON, TOO!
SCHULZ

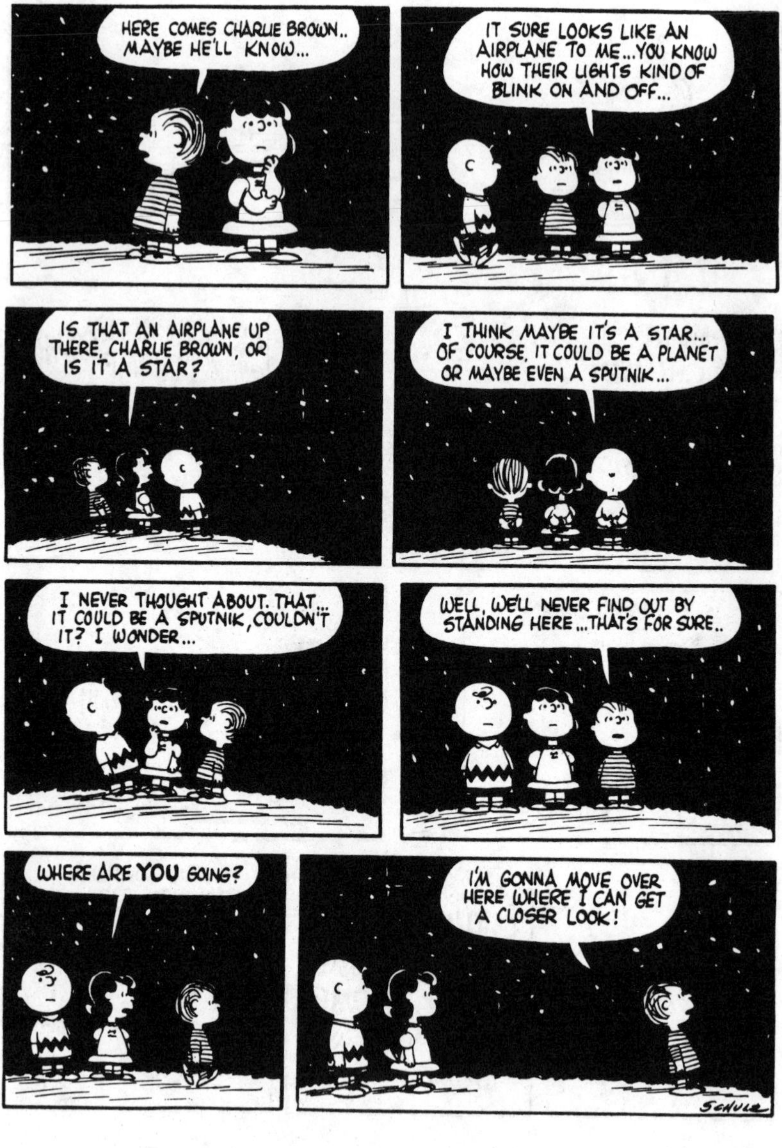
HERE COMES CHARLIE BROWN.. MAYBE HE'LL KNOW...
IT SURE LOOKS LIKE AN AIRPLANE TO ME...YOU KNOW HOW THEIR LIGHTS KIND OF BLINK ON AND OFF...
IS THAT AN AIRPLANE UP THERE, CHARLIE BROWN, OR IS IT A STAR?
I THINK MAYBE IT'S A STAR... OF COURSE, IT COULD BE A PLANET OR MAYBE EVEN A SPUTNIK...
I NEVER THOUGHT ABOUT. THAT... IT COULD BE A SPUTNIK, COULDN'T IT? I WONDER...
WELL, WE'LL NEVER FIND OUT BY STANDING HERE...THAT'S FOR SURE..
WHERE ARE YOU GOING?
I'M GONNA MOVE OVER HERE WHERE I CAN GET A CLOSER LOOK!
SCHULZ

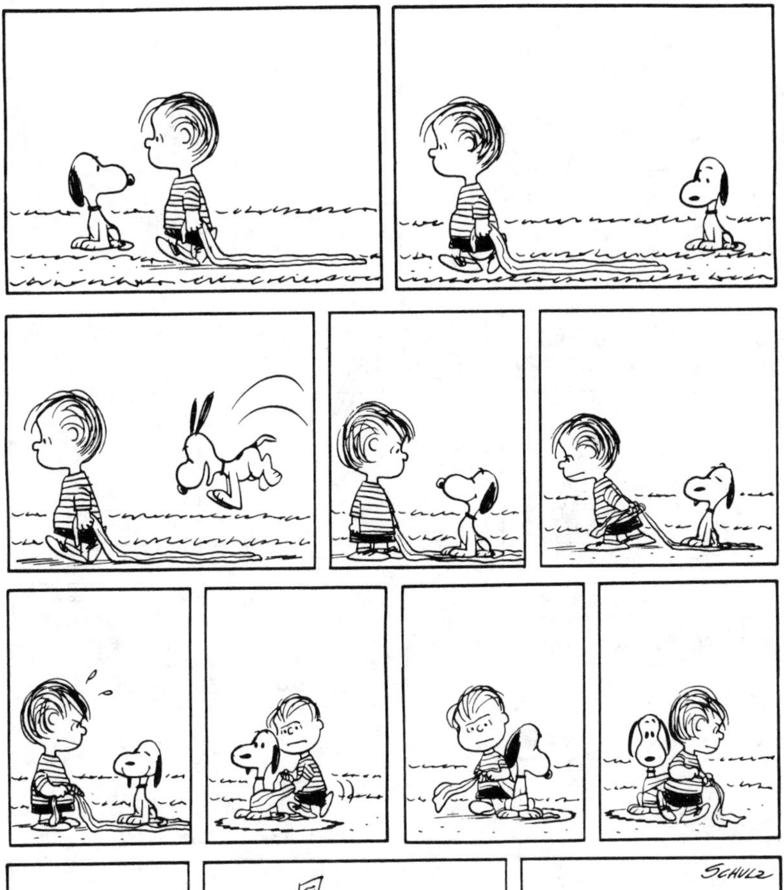
?
ZIP
SCHULZ

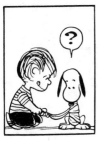

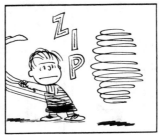

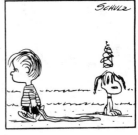

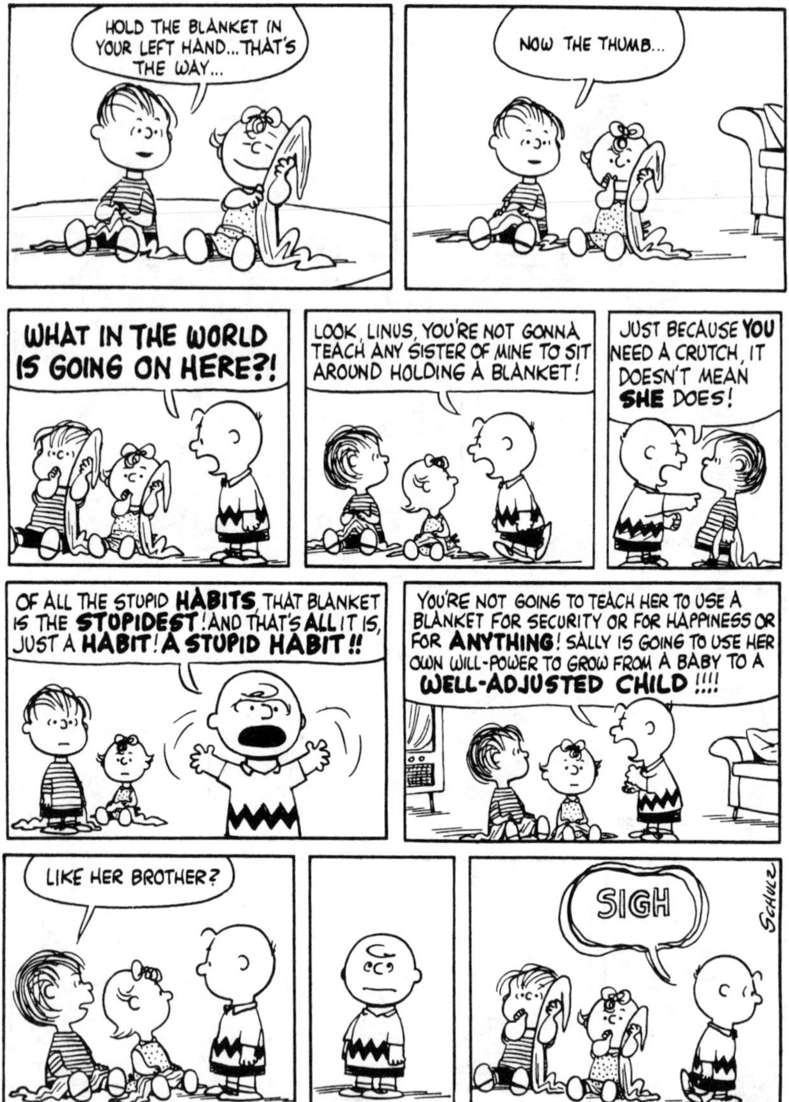
HOLD THE BLANKET IN YOUR LEFT HAND... THAT'S THE WAY...
NOW THE THUMB...
WHAT IN THE WORLD IS GOING ON HERE?!
LOOK, LINUS, YOU'RE NOT GONNA TEACH ANY SISTER OF MINE TO SIT AROUND HOLDING A BLANKET!
JUST BECAUSE YOU NEED A CRUTCH, IT DOESN'T MEAN SHE DOES!
OF ALL THE STUPID HABITS, THAT BLANKET IS THE STOPIDEST! AND THAT'S ALL IT IS, JUST A HABIT! A STUPID HABIT!!
YOU'RE NOT GOING TO TEACH HER TO USE A BLANKET FOR SECURITY OR FOR HAPPINESS OR FOR ANYTHING! SALLY IS GOING TO USE HER OWN WILL-POWER TO GROW FROM A BABY TO A WELL-ADJUSTED CHILD!!!!
LIKE HER BROTHER?
SIGH
SCHULZ

YAWN
CLOMP
WUMP!
?
POOR KID...HE MUST HAVE LOW METABOLISM!
SCHULZ

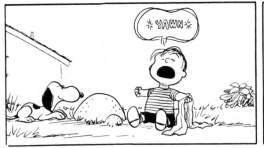

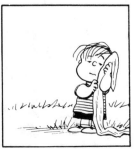

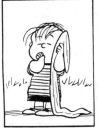

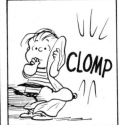

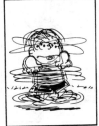

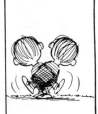

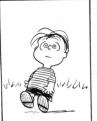

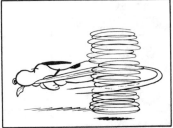

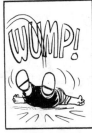

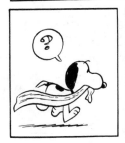

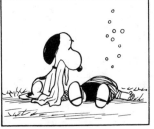

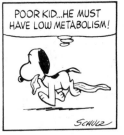

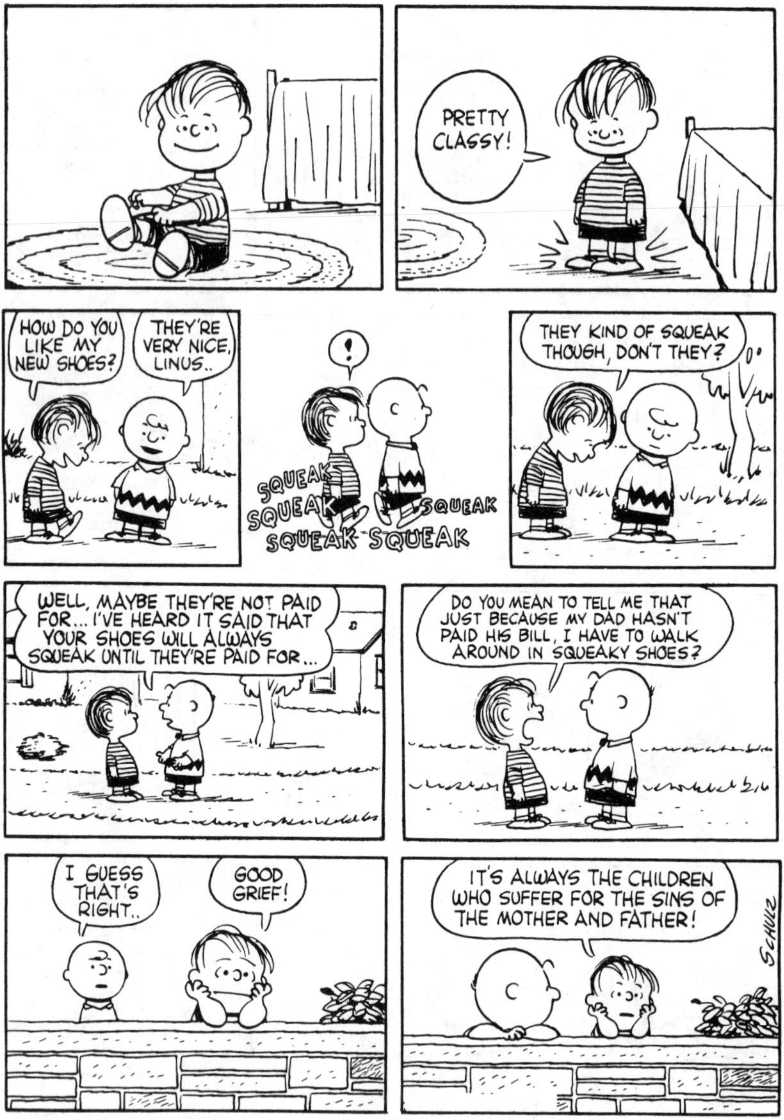

PRETTY CLASSY!
HOW DO YOU LIKE MY NEW SHOES?
THEY'RE VERY NICE, LINUS..
!
SQUEAK SQUEAK SQUEAK SQUEAK SQUEAK
THEY KIND OF SQUEAK THOUGH, DON'T THEY?
WELL, MAYBE THEY'RE NOT PAID FOR... I'VE HEARD IT SAID THAT YOUR SHOES WILL ALWAYS SQUEAK UNTIL THEY'RE PAID FOR...
DO YOU MEAN TO TELL ME THAT JUST BECAUSE MY DAD HASN'T PAID HIS BILL, I HAVE TO WALK AROUND IN SQUEAKY SHOES?
I GUESS THAT'S RIGHT..
GOOD GRIEF!
IT'S ALWAYS THE CHILDREN WHO SUFFER FOR THE SINS OF THE MOTHER AND FATHER!
SCHULZ

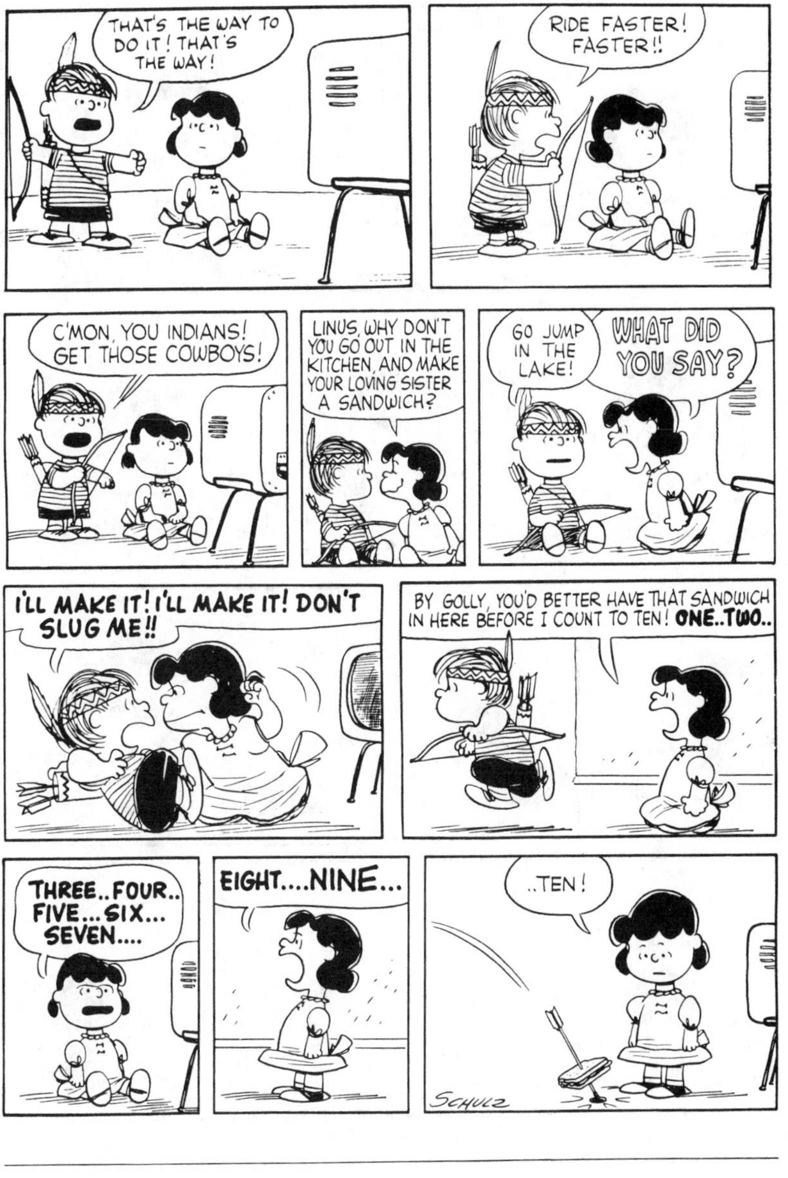

THAT'S THE WAY TO DO IT! THAT'S THE WAY!
RIDE FASTER! FASTER!!
C'MON, YOU INDIANS! GET THOSE COWBOYS!
LINUS, WHY DON'T YOU GO OUT IN THE KITCHEN, AND MAKE YOUR LOVING SISTER A SANDWICH?
GO JUMP IN THE LAKE!
WHAT DID YOU SAY?
I'LL MAKE IT! I'LL MAKE IT! DON'T SLUG ME!!
BY GOLLY, YOU'D BETTER HAVE THAT SANDWICH IN HERE BEFORE I COUNT TO TEN! ONE..TWO..
THREE..FOUR.. FIVE...SIX... SEVEN....
EIGHT....NINE...
..TEN!
SCHULZ

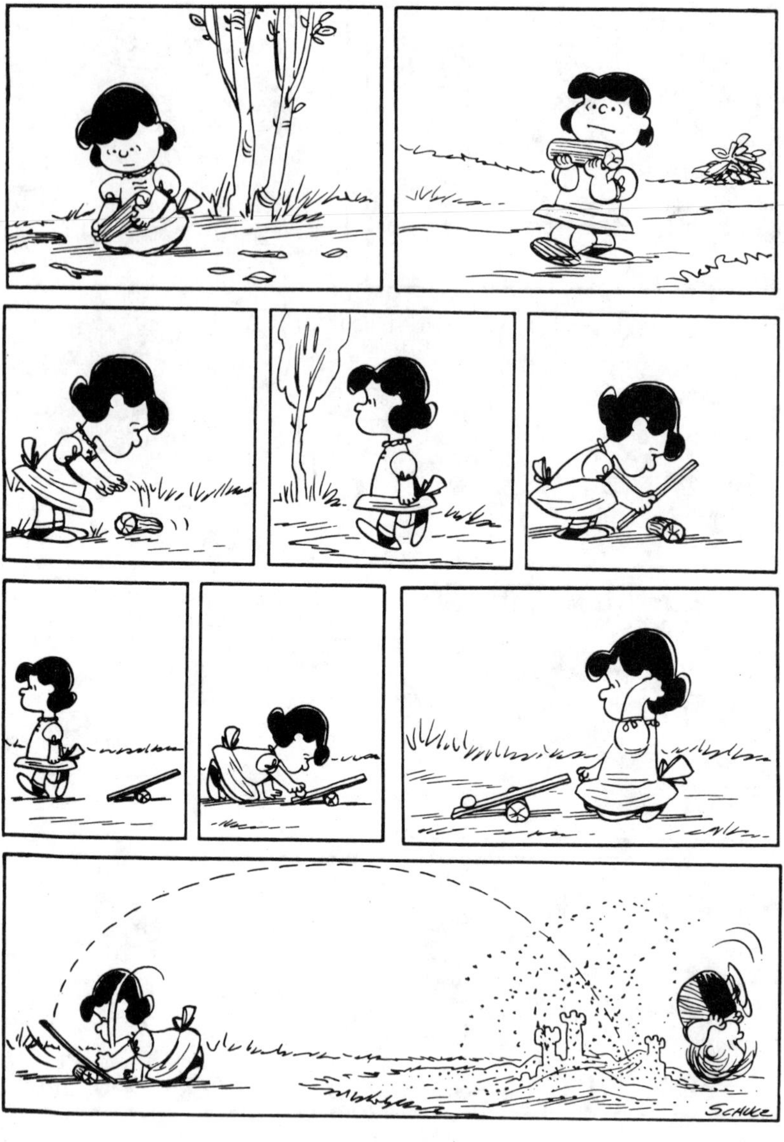
SCHULZ

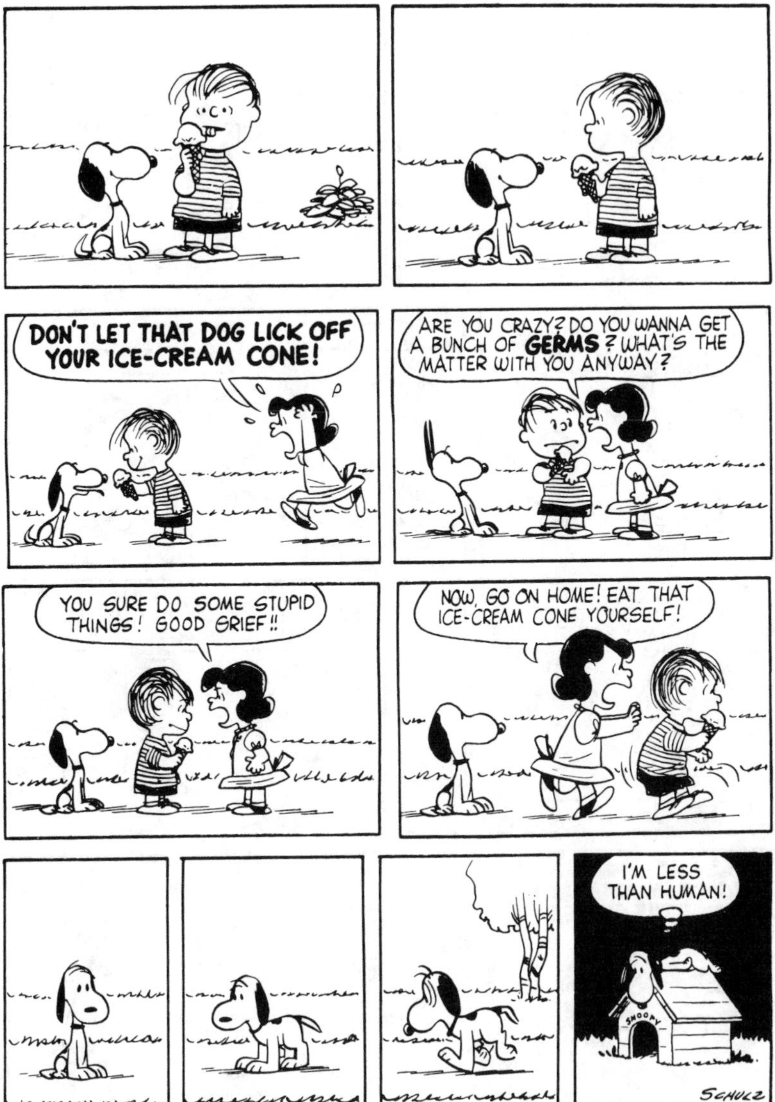
DON'T LET THAT DOG LICK OFF YOUR ICE-CREAM CONE!
ARE YOU CRAZY? DO YOU WANNA GET A BUNCH OF **GERMS**? WHAT'S THE MATTER WITH YOU ANYWAY?
YOU SURE DO SOME STUPID THINGS! GOOD GRIEF!!
NOW, GO ON HOME! EAT THAT ICE-CREAM CONE YOURSELF!
I'M LESS THAN HUMAN!
SNOOPY
SCHULZ

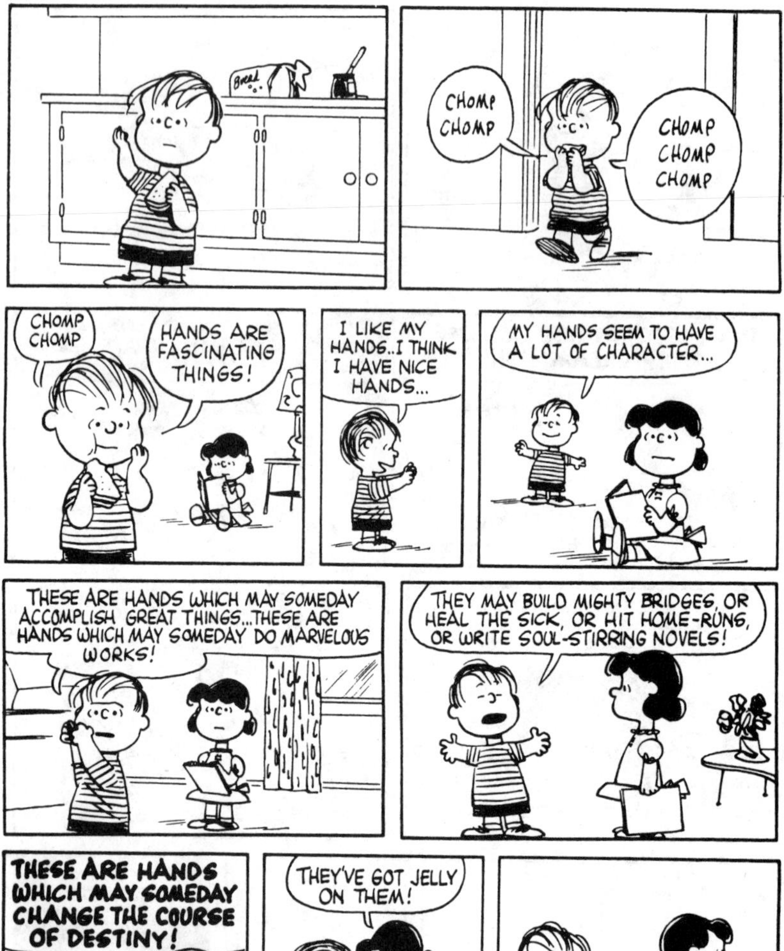
CHOMP CHOMP
CHOMP CHOMP CHOMP
CHOMP CHOMP
HANDS ARE FASCINATING THINGS!
I LIKE MY HANDS..I THINK I HAVE NICE HANDS...
MY HANDS SEEM TO HAVE A LOT OF CHARACTER...
THESE ARE HANDS WHICH MAY SOMEDAY ACCOMPLISH GREAT THINGS...THESE ARE HANDS WHICH MAY SOMEDAY DO MARVELOUS WORKS!
THEY MAY BUILD MIGHTY BRIDGES, OR HEAL THE SICK, OR HIT HOME-RUNS, OR WRITE SOUL-STIRRING NOVELS!
THESE ARE HANDS WHICH MAY SOMEDAY CHANGE THE COURSE OF DESTINY!
THEY'VE GOT JELLY ON THEM!
SCHULZ

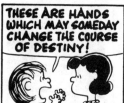

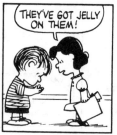

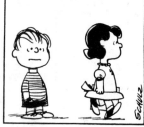

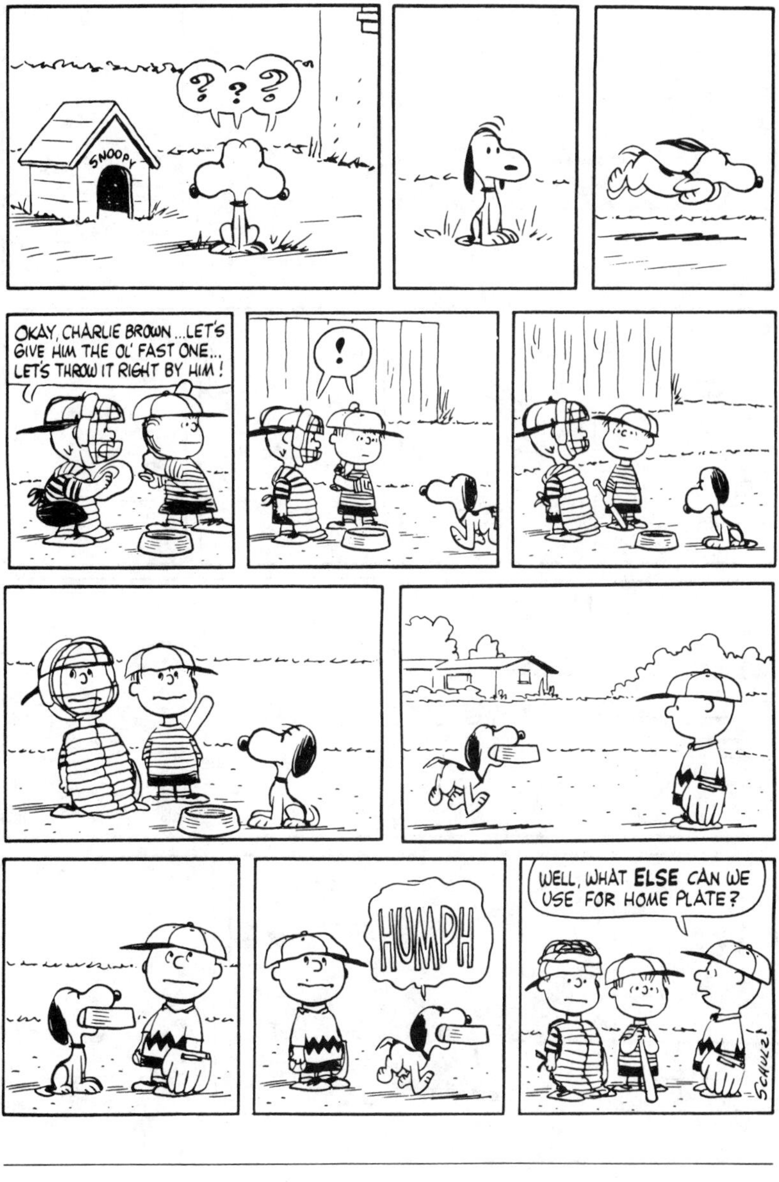
? ? ?
SNOOPY
OKAY, CHARLIE BROWN...LET'S GIVE HIM THE OL' FAST ONE... LET'S THROW IT RIGHT BY HIM!
!
HUMPH
WELL, WHAT ELSE CAN WE USE FOR HOME PLATE?
SCHULZ

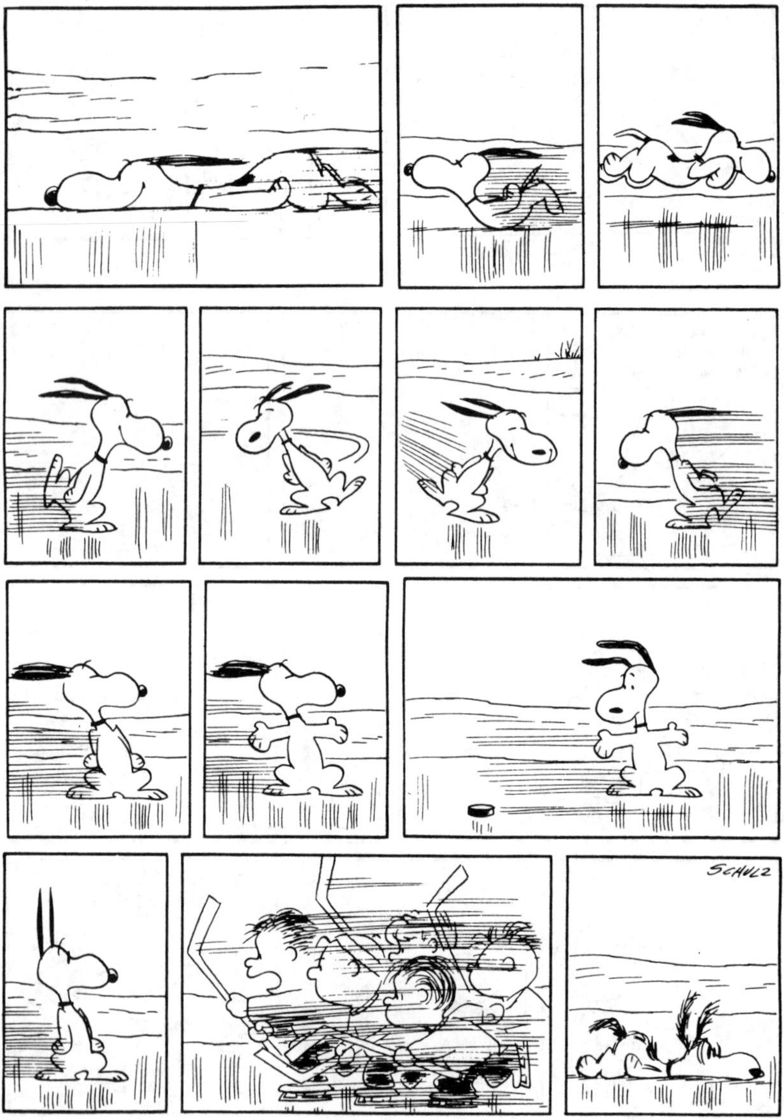
SCHULZ

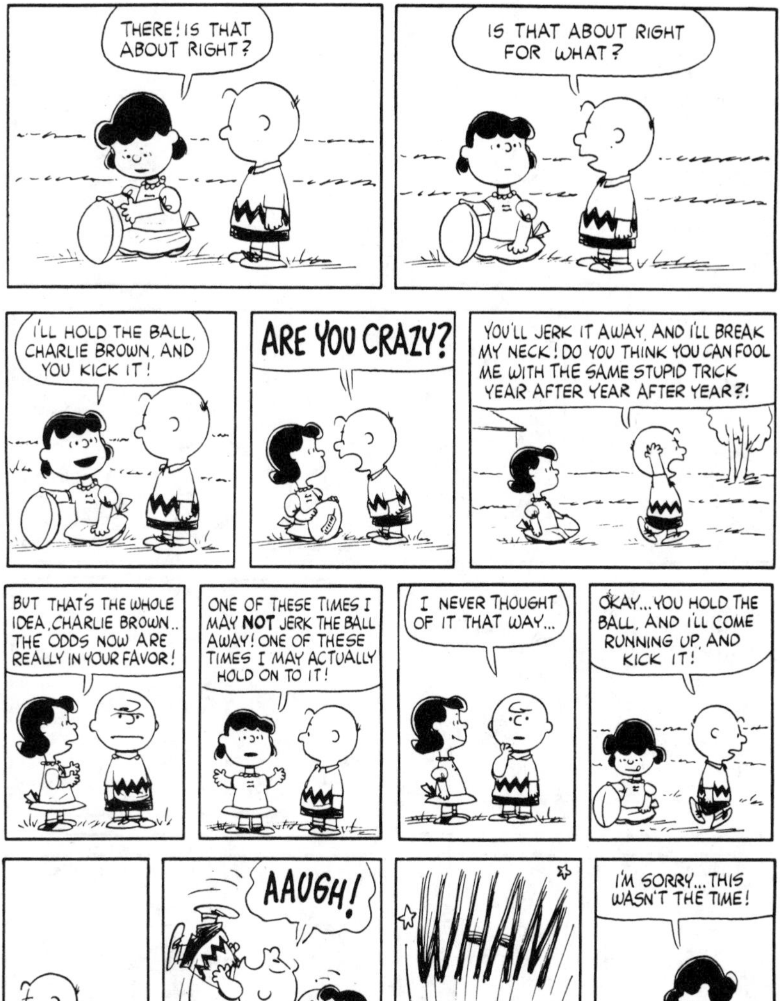
THERE! IS THAT ABOUT RIGHT?
IS THAT ABOUT RIGHT FOR WHAT?
I'LL HOLD THE BALL, CHARLIE BROWN, AND YOU KICK IT!
ARE YOU CRAZY?
YOU'LL JERK IT AWAY, AND I'LL BREAK MY NECK! DO YOU THINK YOU CAN FOOL ME WITH THE SAME STUPID TRICK YEAR AFTER YEAR AFTER YEAR?!
BUT THAT'S THE WHOLE IDEA, CHARLIE BROWN.. THE ODDS NOW ARE REALLY IN YOUR FAVOR!
ONE OF THESE TIMES I MAY NOT JERK THE BALL AWAY! ONE OF THESE TIMES I MAY ACTUALLY HOLD ON TO IT!
I NEVER THOUGHT OF IT THAT WAY...
OKAY... YOU HOLD THE BALL, AND I'LL COME RUNNING UP, AND KICK IT!
AAUGH!
WHAM
I'M SORRY... THIS WASN'T THE TIME!
SCHULZ

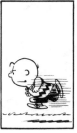

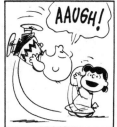

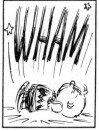

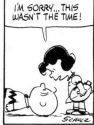

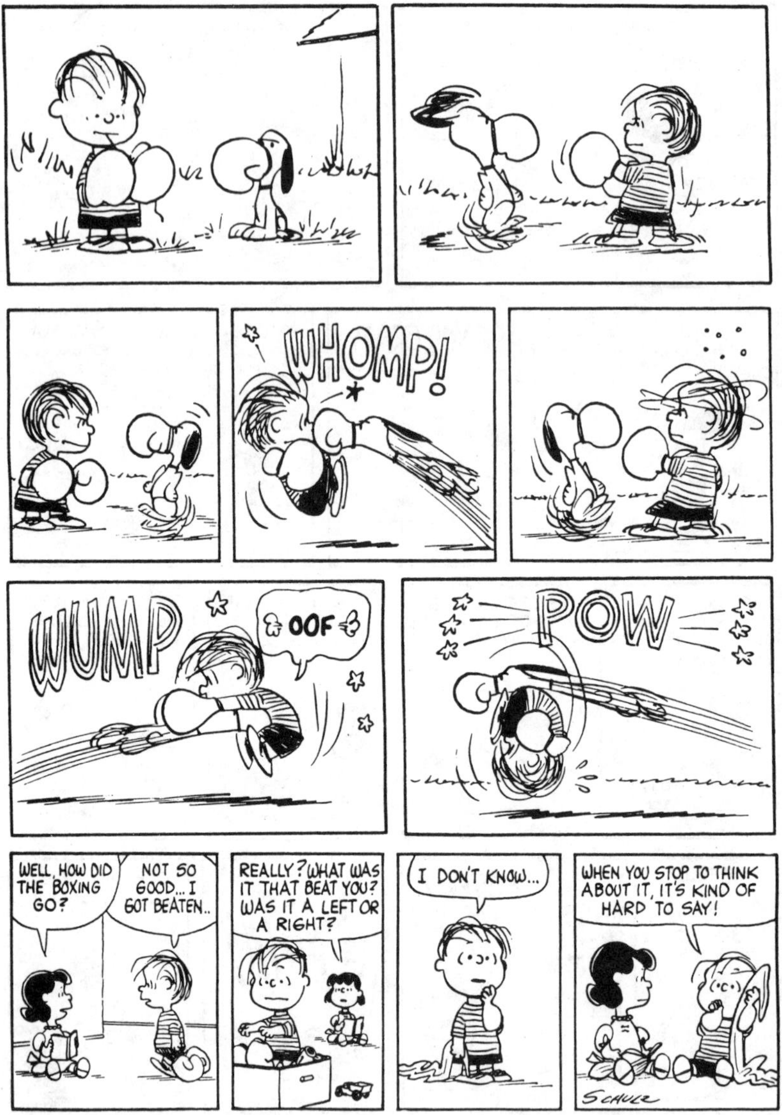
WHOMP!
WUMP
OOF
POW
WELL, HOW DID THE BOXING GO?
NOT SO GOOD... I GOT BEATEN..
REALLY? WHAT WAS IT THAT BEAT YOU? WAS IT A LEFT OR A RIGHT?
I DON'T KNOW...
WHEN YOU STOP TO THINK ABOUT IT, IT'S KIND OF HARD TO SAY!
SCHULZ

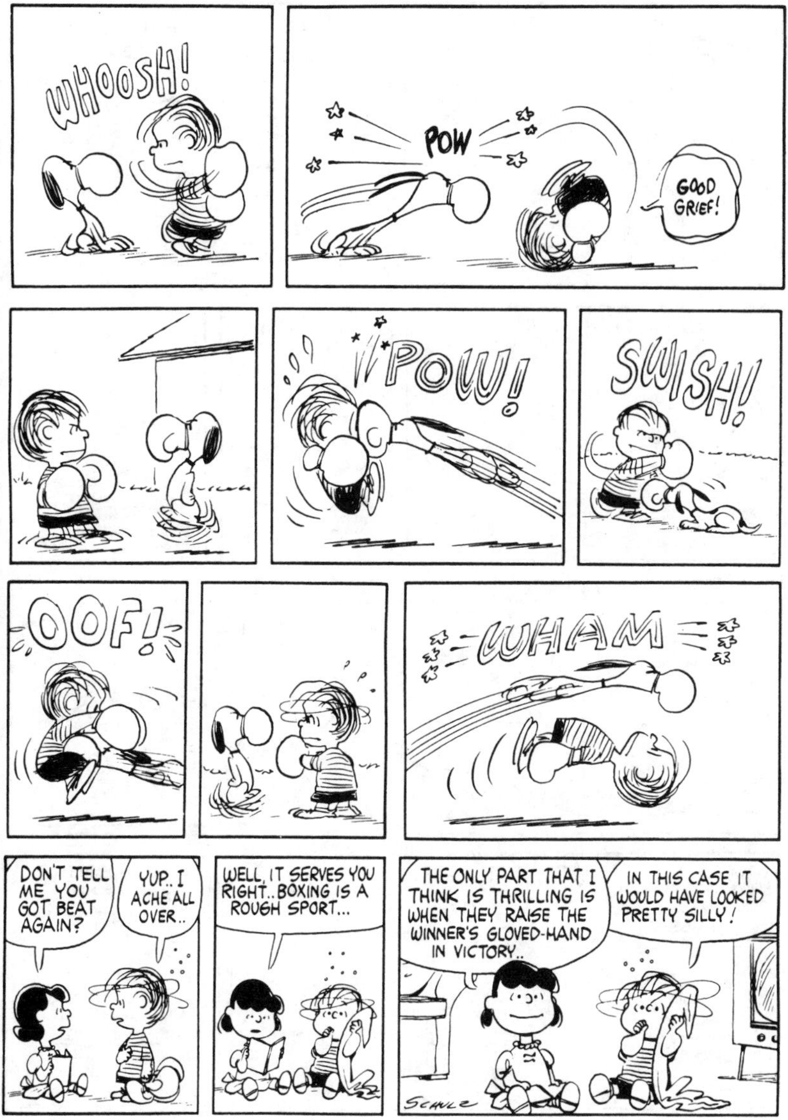
WHOOSH!
POW
GOOD GRIEF!
POW!
SWISH!
OOF!
WHAM
DON'T TELL ME YOU GOT BEAT AGAIN?
YUP.. I ACHE ALL OVER..
WELL, IT SERVES YOU RIGHT.. BOXING IS A ROUGH SPORT...
THE ONLY PART THAT I THINK IS THRILLING IS WHEN THEY RAISE THE WINNER'S GLOVED-HAND IN VICTORY..
IN THIS CASE IT WOULD HAVE LOOKED PRETTY SILLY!
SCHULZ

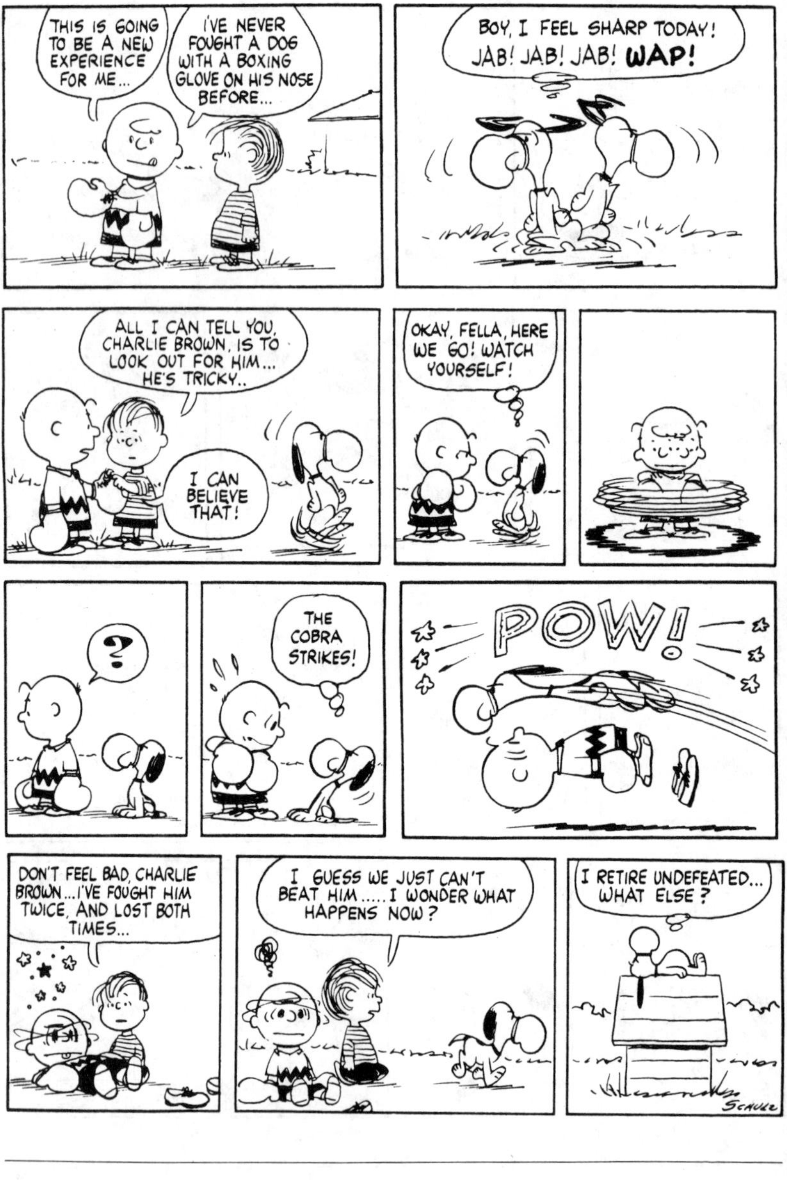
THIS IS GOING TO BE A NEW EXPERIENCE FOR ME...
I'VE NEVER FOUGHT A DOG WITH A BOXING GLOVE ON HIS NOSE BEFORE...
BOY, I FEEL SHARP TODAY! JAB! JAB! JAB! WAP!
ALL I CAN TELL YOU, CHARLIE BROWN, IS TO LOOK OUT FOR HIM... HE'S TRICKY..
I CAN BELIEVE THAT!
OKAY, FELLA, HERE WE GO! WATCH YOURSELF!
?
THE COBRA STRIKES!
POW!
DON'T FEEL BAD, CHARLIE BROWN...I'VE FOUGHT HIM TWICE, AND LOST BOTH TIMES...
I GUESS WE JUST CAN'T BEAT HIM..... I WONDER WHAT HAPPENS NOW?
I RETIRE UNDEFEATED... WHAT ELSE?
SCHULZ

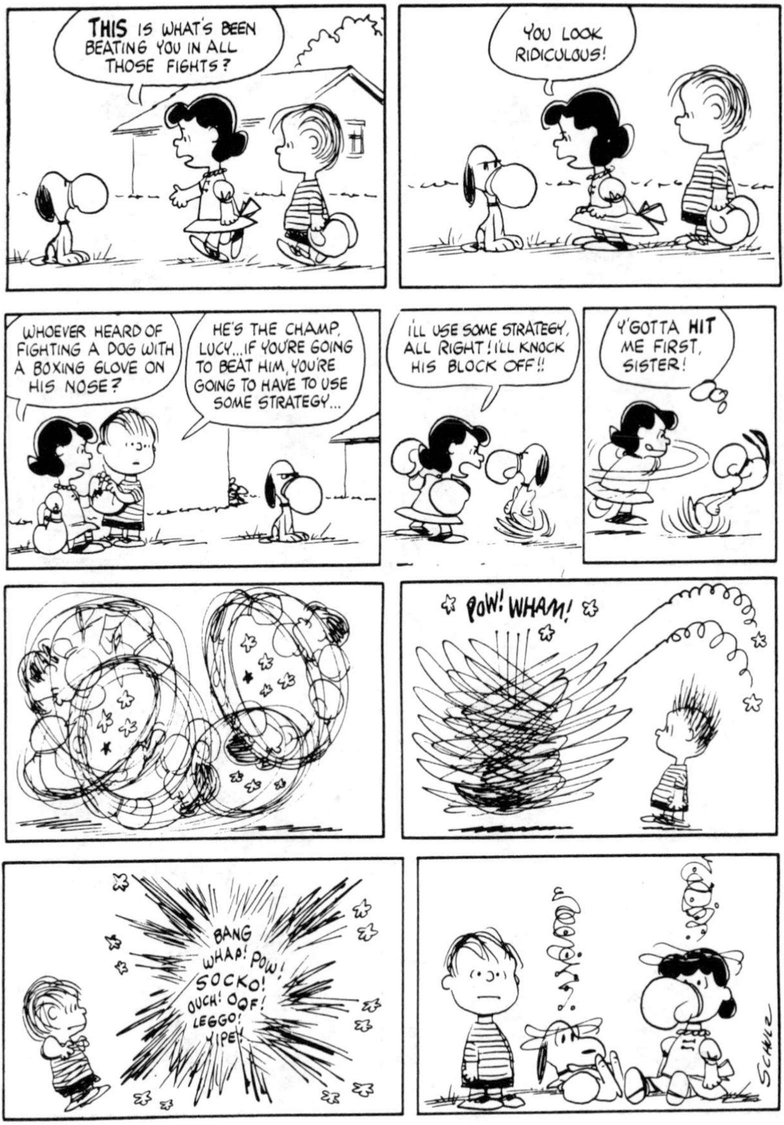
THIS IS WHAT'S BEEN BEATING YOU IN ALL THOSE FIGHTS?
YOU LOOK RIDICULOUS!
WHOEVER HEARD OF FIGHTING A DOG WITH A BOXING GLOVE ON HIS NOSE?
HE'S THE CHAMP, LUCY...IF YOU'RE GOING TO BEAT HIM, YOU'RE GOING TO HAVE TO USE SOME STRATEGY...
I'LL USE SOME STRATEGY, ALL RIGHT! I'LL KNOCK HIS BLOCK OFF!!
Y'GOTTA HIT ME FIRST, SISTER!
POW! WHAM!
BANG
WHAP! POW!
SOCKO!
OUCH! OOF!
LEGGO!
YIPE!
SCHULZ

IF YOU THINK YOU'RE GETTING AWAY WITH SOMETHING, YOU'RE MISTAKEN!
YOU'RE NOT INSCRUTABLE, YOU KNOW!
YOU CAN'T PUT ANYTHING OVER ON ME!
I KNOW JUST WHAT YOU'RE THINKING!
I CAN SEE RIGHT THROUGH YOU! YOU'RE TRANSPARENT!!
SIGH
I HAVE A GLASS HEAD!
SCHULZ

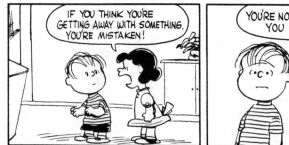

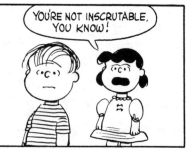

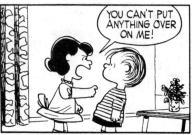

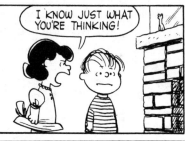

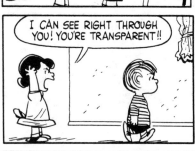

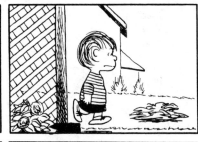

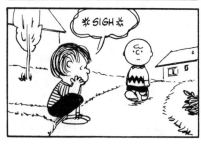

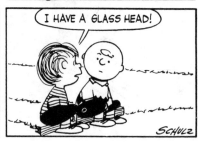

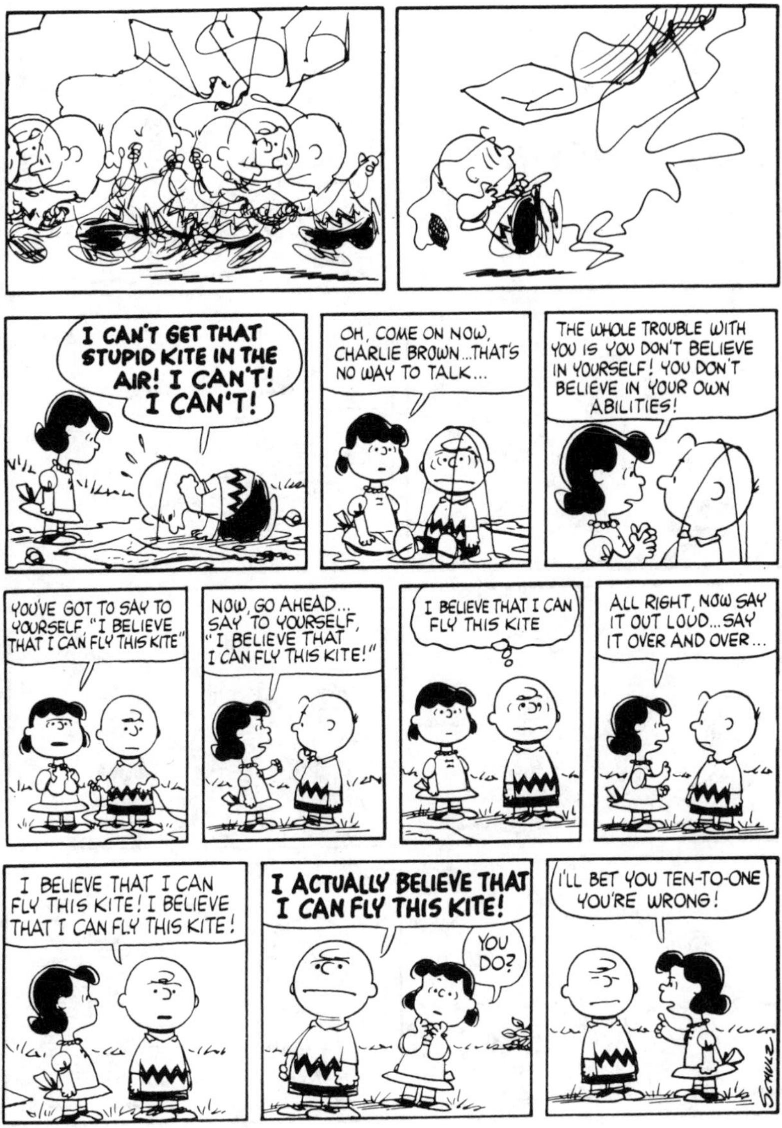

I CAN'T GET THAT STUPID KITE IN THE AIR! I CAN'T! I CAN'T!
OH, COME ON NOW, CHARLIE BROWN...THAT'S NO WAY TO TALK...
THE WHOLE TROUBLE WITH YOU IS YOU DON'T BELIEVE IN YOURSELF! YOU DON'T BELIEVE IN YOUR OWN ABILITIES!
YOU'VE GOT TO SAY TO YOURSELF, "I BELIEVE THAT I CAN FLY THIS KITE"
NOW, GO AHEAD... SAY TO YOURSELF, "I BELIEVE THAT I CAN FLY THIS KITE!"
I BELIEVE THAT I CAN FLY THIS KITE
ALL RIGHT, NOW SAY IT OUT LOUD...SAY IT OVER AND OVER...
I BELIEVE THAT I CAN FLY THIS KITE! I BELIEVE THAT I CAN FLY THIS KITE!
I ACTUALLY BELIEVE THAT I CAN FLY THIS KITE!
YOU DO?
I'LL BET YOU TEN-TO-ONE YOU'RE WRONG!
SCHULZ

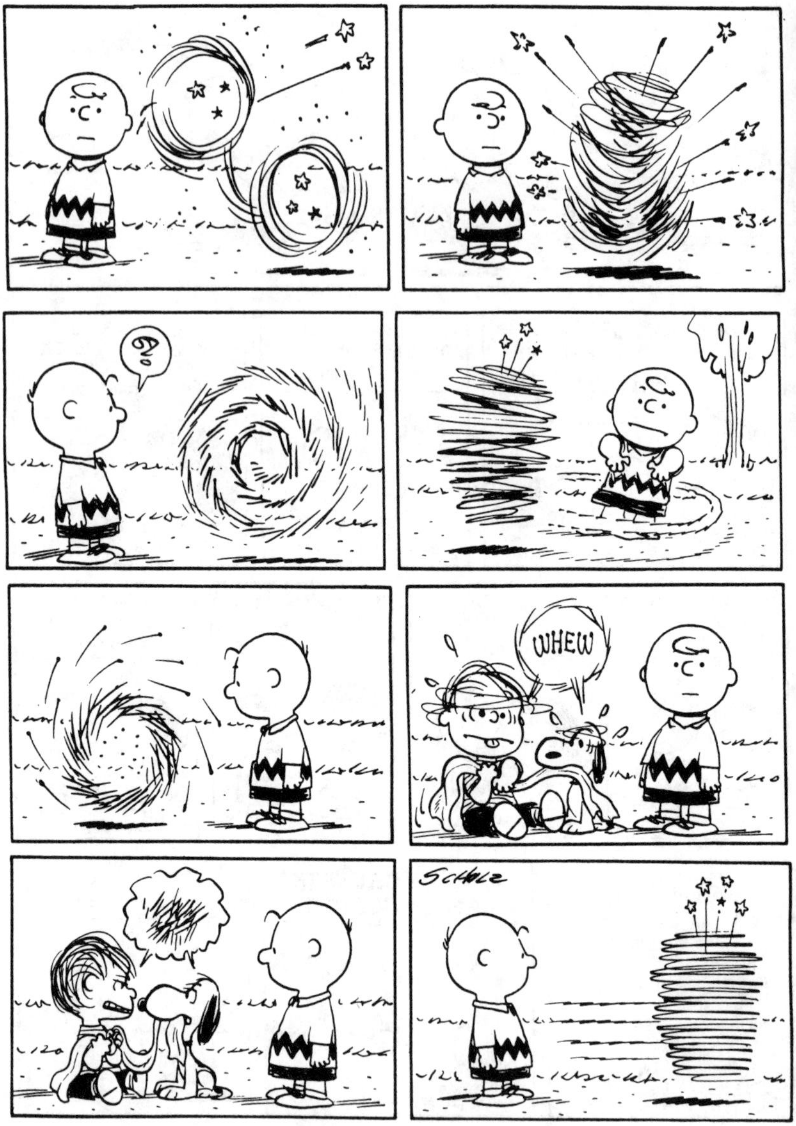
WHEW
SCHULZ

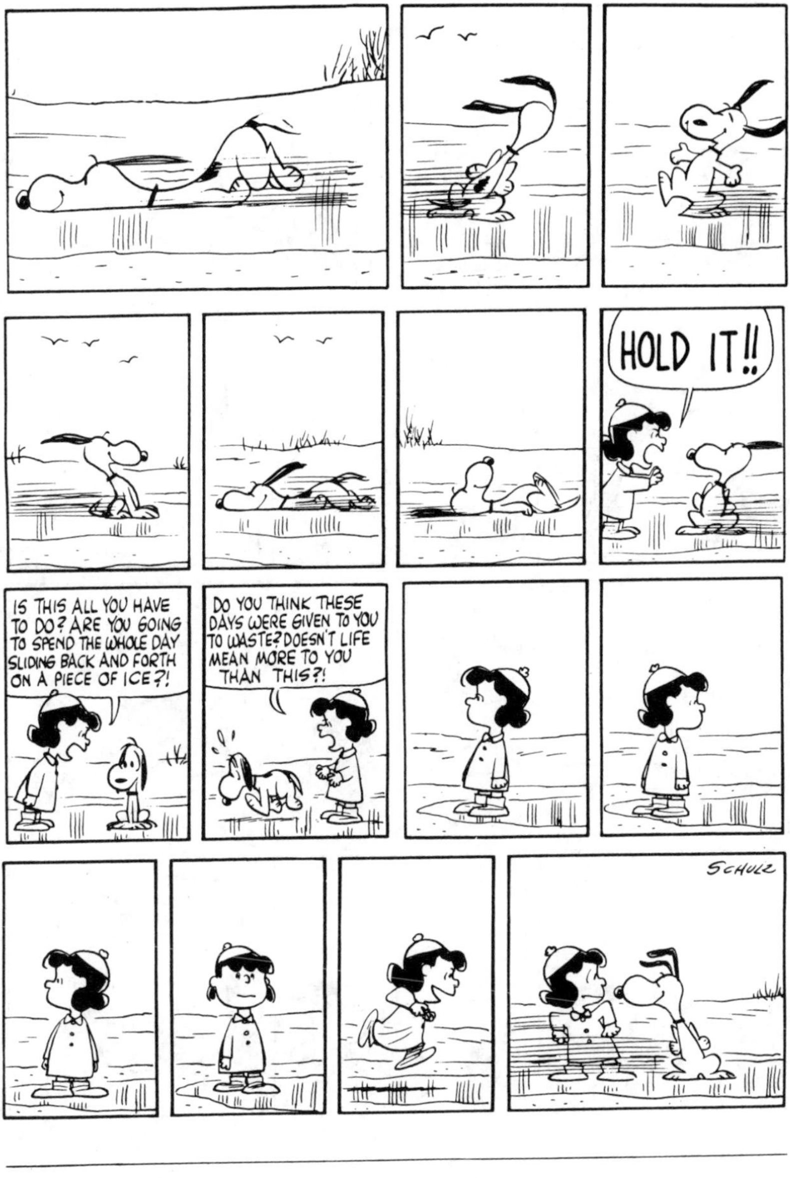
HOLD IT!!
IS THIS ALL YOU HAVE TO DO? ARE YOU GOING TO SPEND THE WHOLE DAY SLIDING BACK AND FORTH ON A PIECE OF ICE?!
DO YOU THINK THESE DAYS WERE GIVEN TO YOU TO WASTE? DOESN'T LIFE MEAN MORE TO YOU THAN THIS?!
SCHULZ

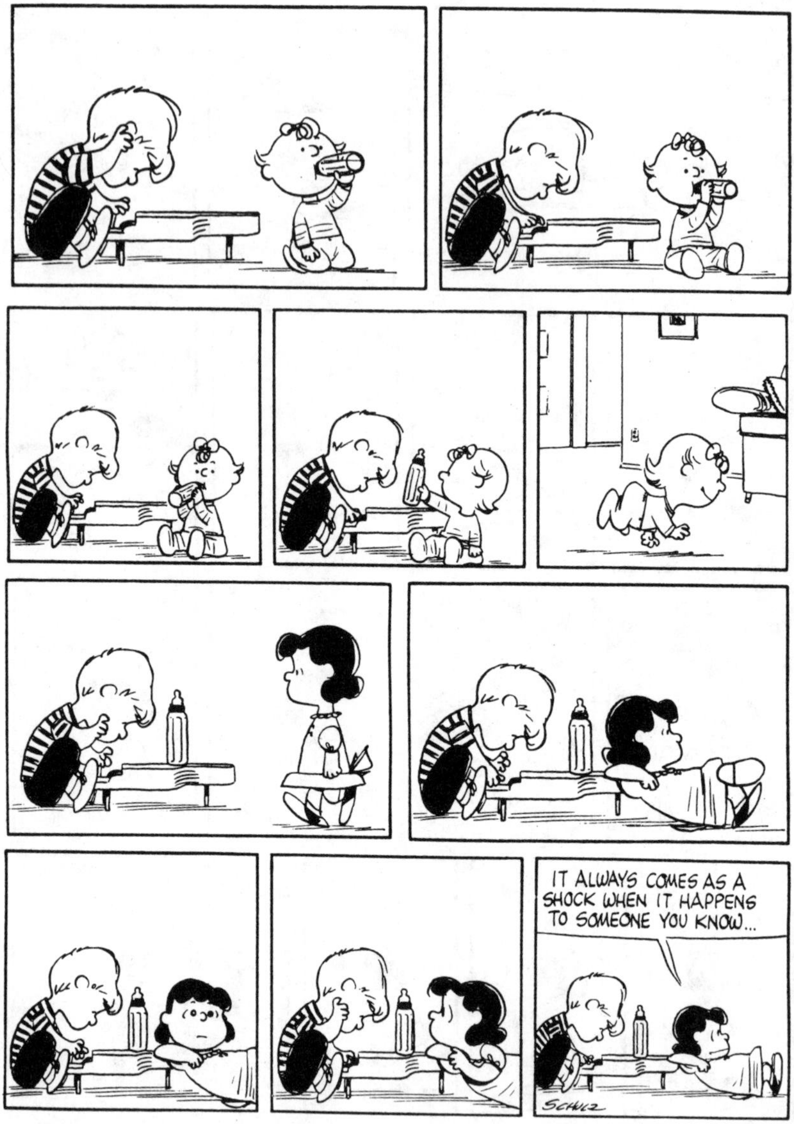

IT ALWAYS COMES AS A SHOCK WHEN IT HAPPENS TO SOMEONE YOU KNOW...
SCHULZ

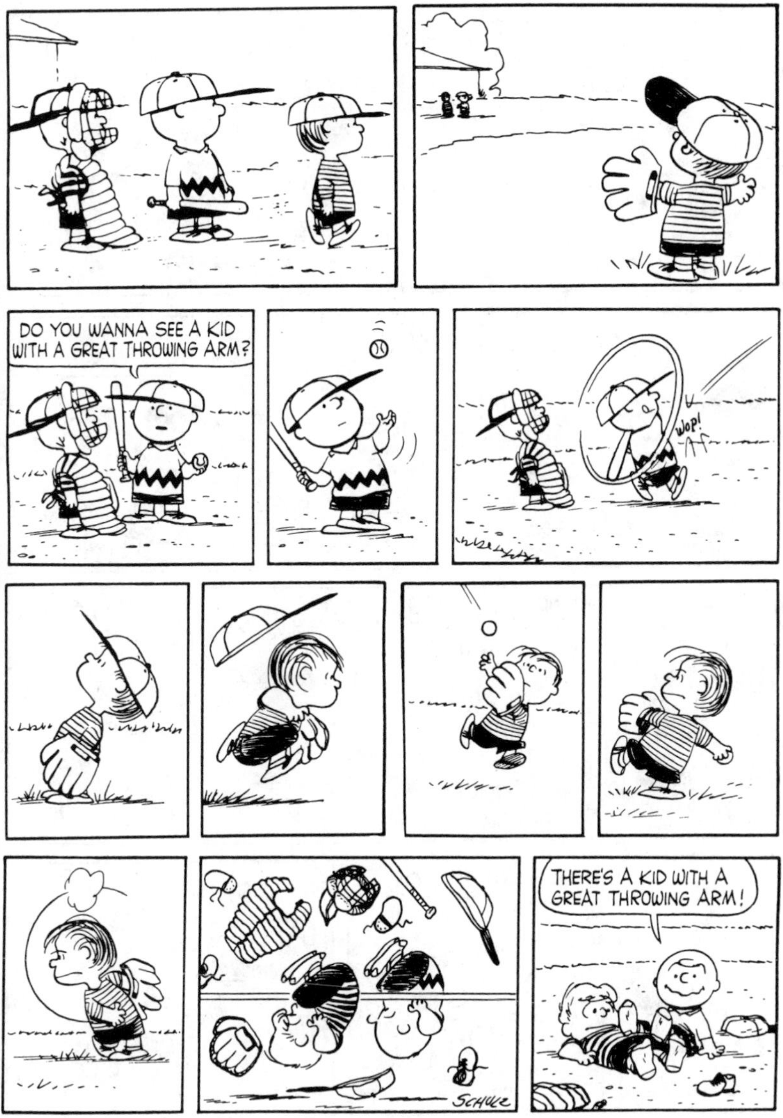
DO YOU WANNA SEE A KID WITH A GREAT THROWING ARM?
WOP!
SCHULZ
THERE'S A KID WITH A GREAT THROWING ARM!

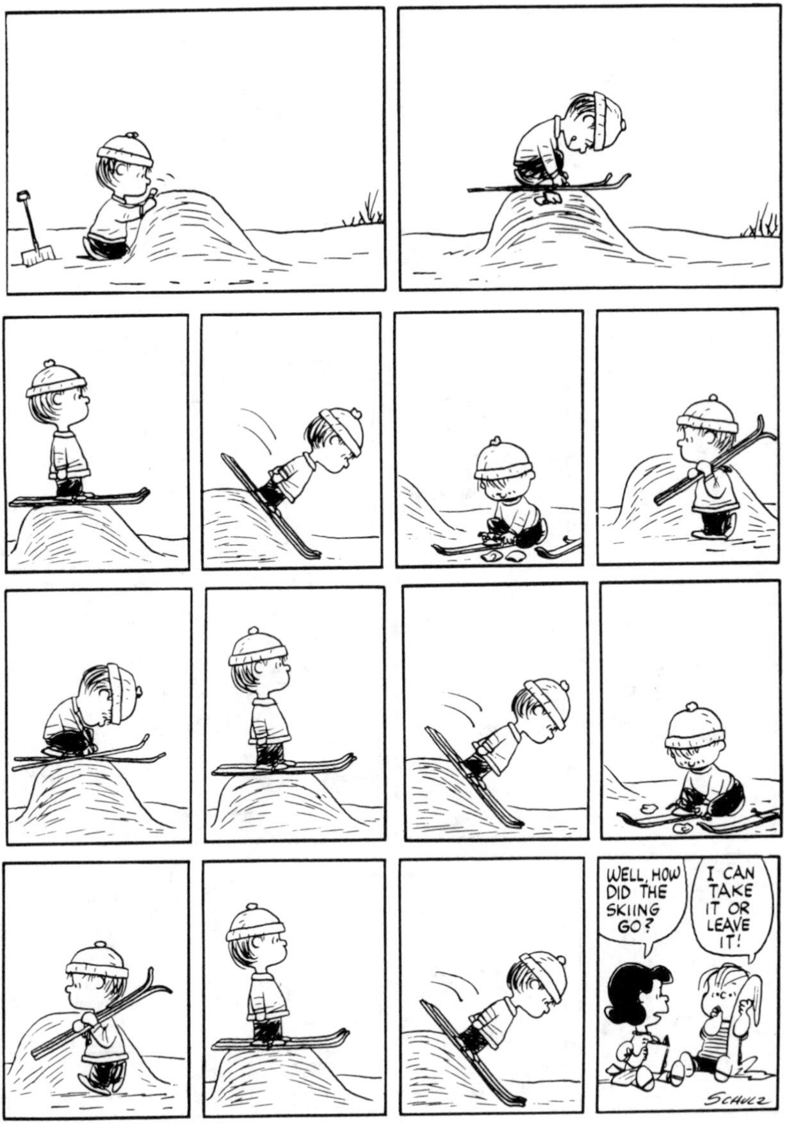
WELL, HOW DID THE SKIING GO?
I CAN TAKE IT OR LEAVE IT!
SCHULZ

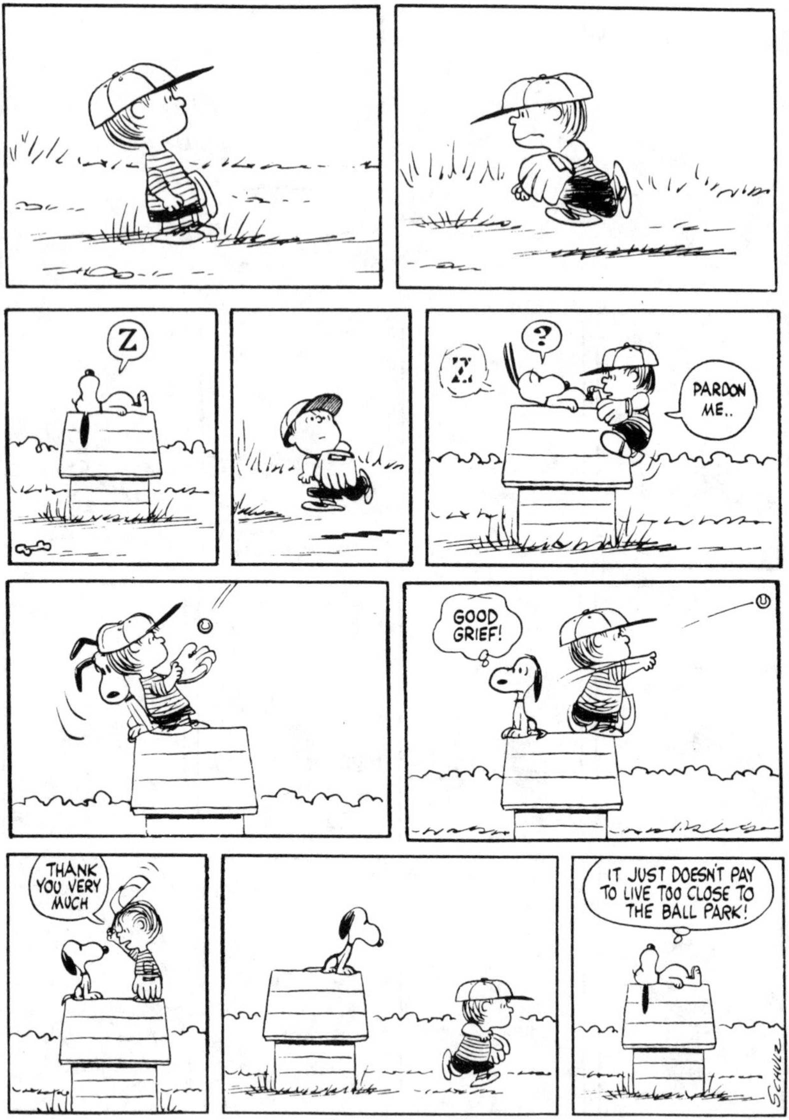
Z
?
Z
PARDON ME..
GOOD GRIEF!
THANK YOU VERY MUCH
IT JUST DOESN'T PAY TO LIVE TOO CLOSE TO THE BALL PARK!
SCHULZ

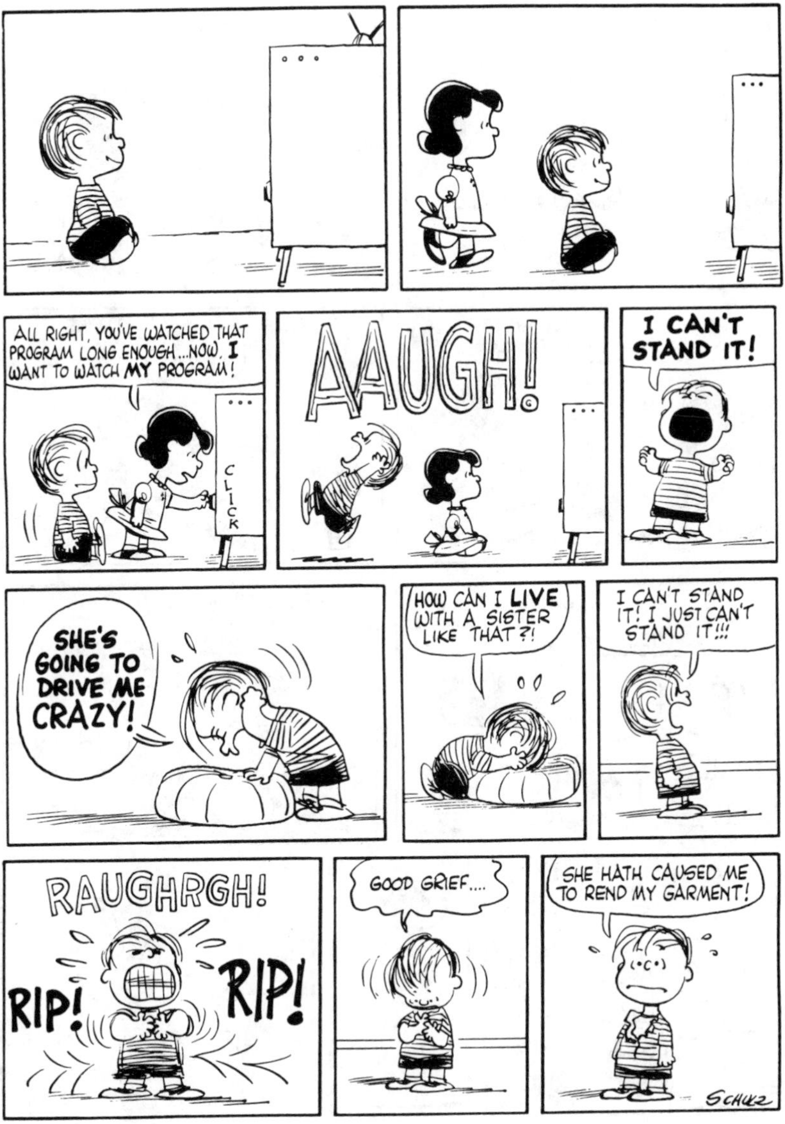
ALL RIGHT, YOU'VE WATCHED THAT PROGRAM LONG ENOUGH...NOW, I WANT TO WATCH MY PROGRAM!
CLICK
AAUGH!
I CAN'T STAND IT!
SHE'S GOING TO DRIVE ME CRAZY!
HOW CAN I LIVE WITH A SISTER LIKE THAT?!
I CAN'T STAND IT! I JUST CAN'T STAND IT!!!
RAUGHRGH!
RIP!
RIP!
GOOD GRIEF....
SHE HATH CAUSED ME TO REND MY GARMENT!
SCHULZ

YOU AND THAT STUPID BLANKET!
HI, BOYS!
HOW DO YOU LIKE MY HAIR THIS WAY, CHARLIE BROWN?
IT LOOKS REAL NICE, VIOLET
I'M GLAD YOU LIKE IT... I WAS GETTING A LITTLE TIRED OF THAT PONY TAIL..
WELL, I THINK IT'S LOVELY THIS WAY...IT'S VERY BECOMING..
THANK YOU
"WELL, I THINK IT'S LOVELY THIS WAY...IT'S VERY BECOMING"
HA HA HA H HA HA HA A H HA H H
SCHULZ

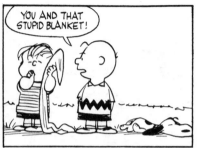

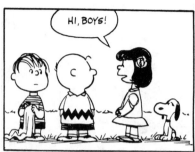

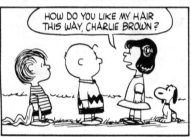

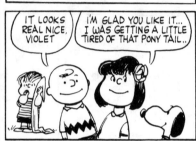

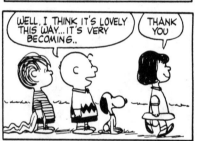

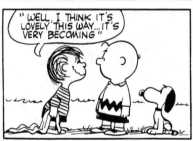

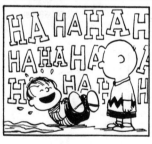

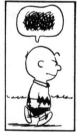

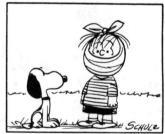

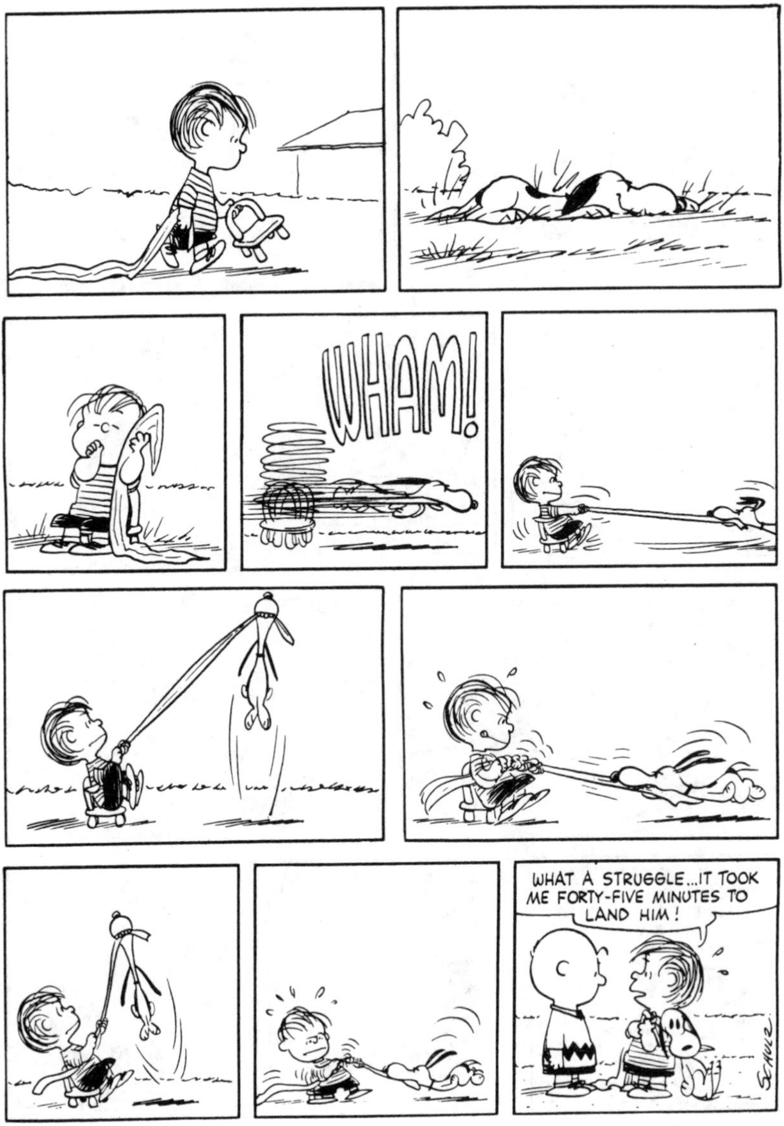
WHAM!
WHAT A STRUGGLE...IT TOOK ME FORTY-FIVE MINUTES TO LAND HIM!
SCHULZ

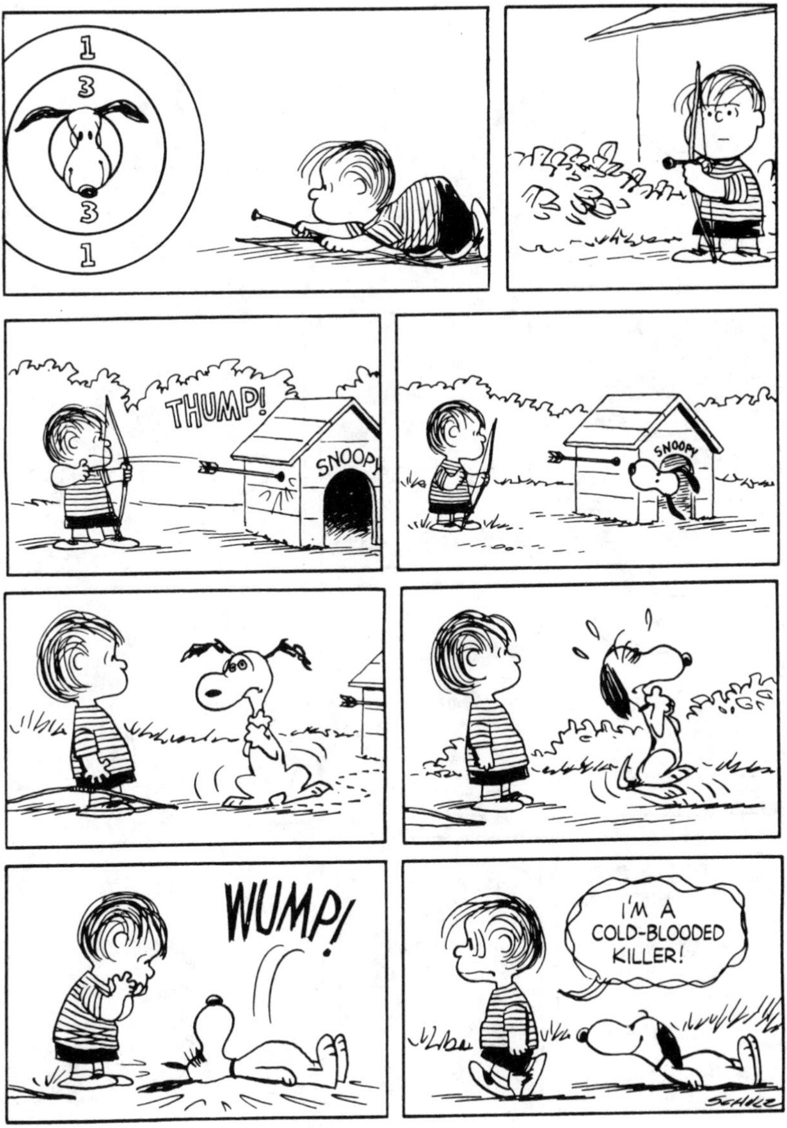

1
3
3
1
THUMP!
SNOOPY
SNOOPY
WUMP!
I'M A COLD-BLOODED KILLER!
SCHULZ

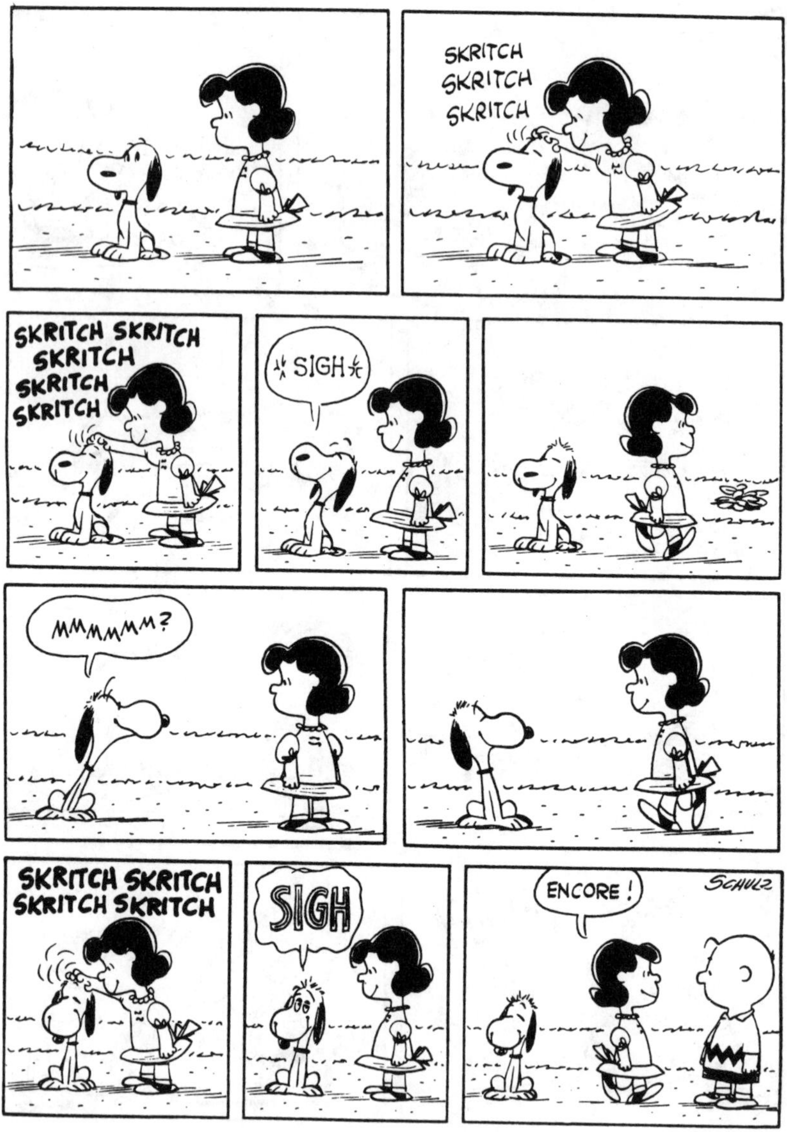
SKRITCH
SKRITCH
SKRITCH
SKRITCH SKRITCH
SKRITCH
SKRITCH
SKRITCH
SIGH
MMMMMM?
SKRITCH SKRITCH
SKRITCH SKRITCH
SIGH
ENCORE!
SCHULZ

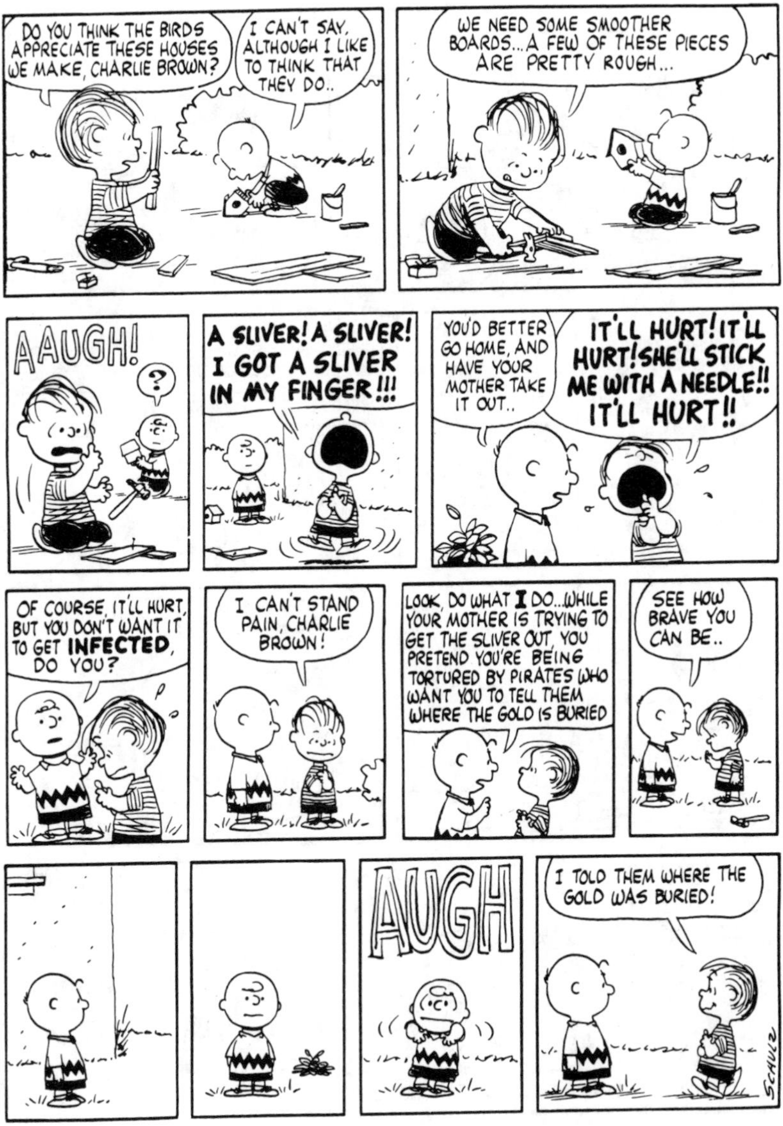
DO YOU THINK THE BIRDS APPRECIATE THESE HOUSES WE MAKE, CHARLIE BROWN?
I CAN'T SAY, ALTHOUGH I LIKE TO THINK THAT THEY DO..
WE NEED SOME SMOOTHER BOARDS...A FEW OF THESE PIECES ARE PRETTY ROUGH...
AAUGH!
?
A SLIVER! A SLIVER! I GOT A SLIVER IN MY FINGER!!!
YOU'D BETTER GO HOME, AND HAVE YOUR MOTHER TAKE IT OUT..
IT'LL HURT! IT'LL HURT! SHE'LL STICK ME WITH A NEEDLE!! IT'LL HURT!!
OF COURSE, IT'LL HURT, BUT YOU DON'T WANT IT TO GET INFECTED, DO YOU?
I CAN'T STAND PAIN, CHARLIE BROWN!
LOOK, DO WHAT I DO...WHILE YOUR MOTHER IS TRYING TO GET THE SLIVER OUT, YOU PRETEND YOU'RE BEING TORTURED BY PIRATES WHO WANT YOU TO TELL THEM WHERE THE GOLD IS BURIED
SEE HOW BRAVE YOU CAN BE..
AUGH
I TOLD THEM WHERE THE GOLD WAS BURIED!
SCHULZ

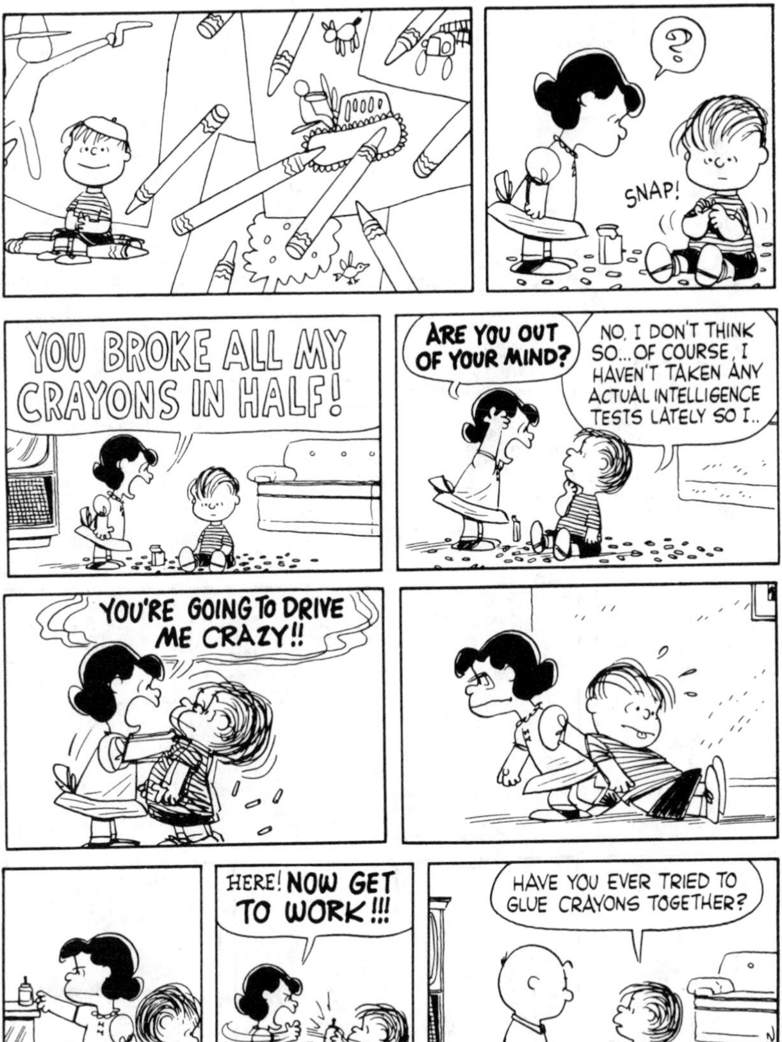
?
SNAP!
YOU BROKE ALL MY CRAYONS IN HALF!
ARE YOU OUT OF YOUR MIND?
NO, I DON'T THINK SO...OF COURSE, I HAVEN'T TAKEN ANY ACTUAL INTELLIGENCE TESTS LATELY SO I..
YOU'RE GOING TO DRIVE ME CRAZY!!
HERE! NOW GET TO WORK!!!
HAVE YOU EVER TRIED TO GLUE CRAYONS TOGETHER?
SCHULZ

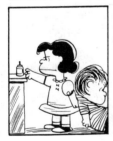

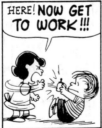

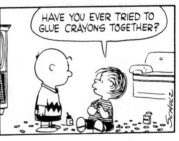

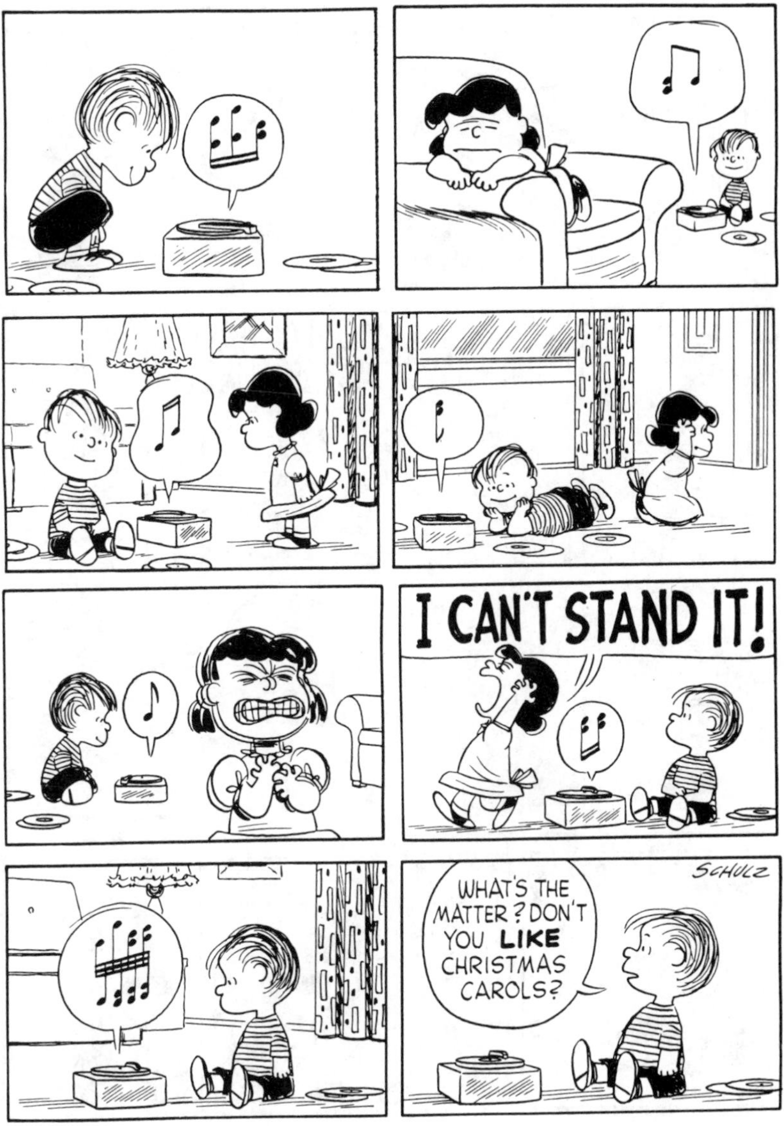
I CAN'T STAND IT!
SCHULZ
WHAT'S THE MATTER? DON'T YOU LIKE CHRISTMAS CAROLS?

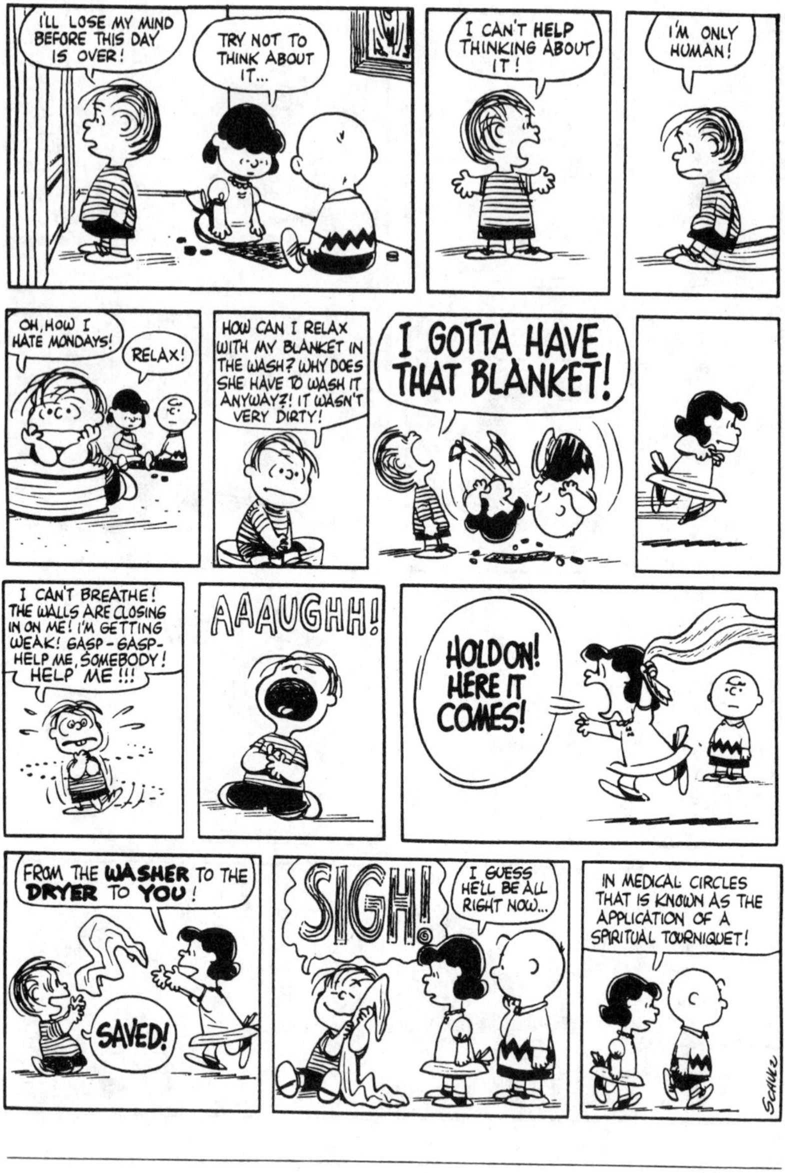

I'LL LOSE MY MIND BEFORE THIS DAY IS OVER!
TRY NOT TO THINK ABOUT IT...
I CAN'T HELP THINKING ABOUT IT!
I'M ONLY HUMAN!
OH, HOW I HATE MONDAYS!
RELAX!
HOW CAN I RELAX WITH MY BLANKET IN THE WASH? WHY DOES SHE HAVE TO WASH IT ANYWAY?! IT WASN'T VERY DIRTY!
I GOTTA HAVE THAT BLANKET!
I CAN'T BREATHE! THE WALLS ARE CLOSING IN ON ME! I'M GETTING WEAK! GASP-GASP-HELP ME, SOMEBODY! HELP ME!!!
AAAUGHH!
HOLDON! HERE IT COMES!
FROM THE WASHER TO THE DRYER TO YOU!
SAVED!
SIGH!
I GUESS HE'LL BE ALL RIGHT NOW...
IN MEDICAL CIRCLES THAT IS KNOWN AS THE APPLICATION OF A SPIRITUAL TOURNIQUET!
SCHULZ

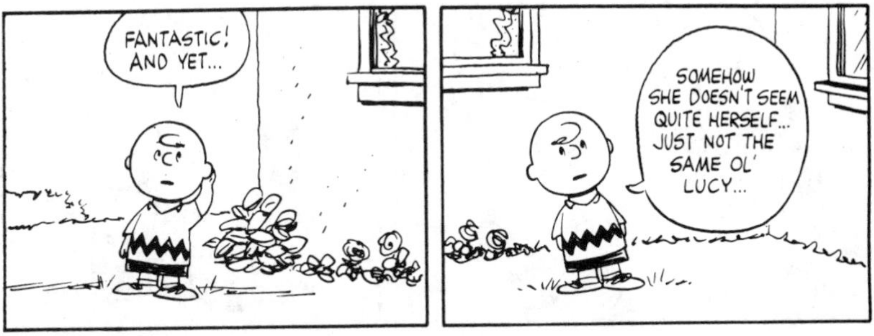
FANTASTIC! AND YET...
SOMEHOW SHE DOESN'T SEEM QUITE HERSELF... JUST NOT THE SAME OL' LUCY...

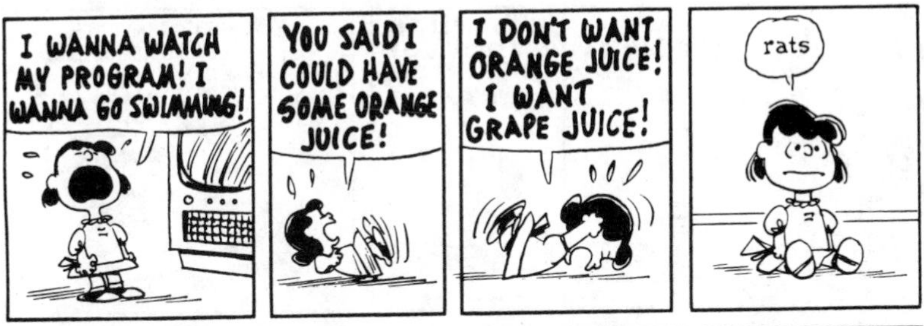
I WANNA WATCH MY PROGRAM! I WANNA GO SWIMMING!
YOU SAID I COULD HAVE SOME ORANGE JUICE!
I DON'T WANT ORANGE JUICE! I WANT GRAPE JUICE!
rats

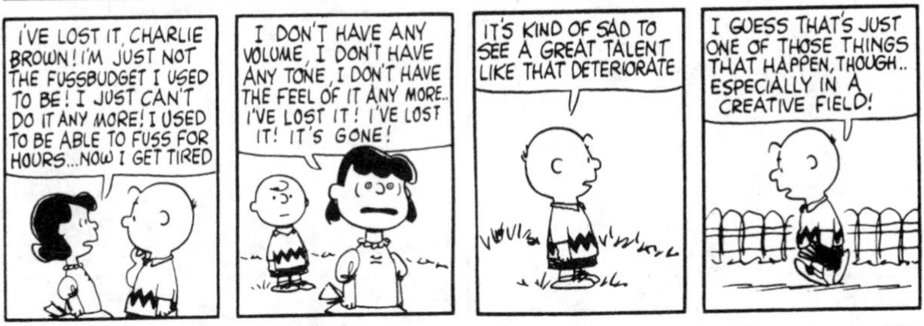
I'VE LOST IT, CHARLIE BROWN! I'M JUST NOT THE FUSSBUDGET I USED TO BE! I JUST CAN'T DO IT ANY MORE! I USED TO BE ABLE TO FUSS FOR HOURS...NOW I GET TIRED
I DON'T HAVE ANY VOLUME, I DON'T HAVE ANY TONE, I DON'T HAVE THE FEEL OF IT ANY MORE.. I'VE LOST IT! I'VE LOST IT! IT'S GONE!
IT'S KIND OF SAD TO SEE A GREAT TALENT LIKE THAT DETERIORATE
I GUESS THAT'S JUST ONE OF THOSE THINGS THAT HAPPEN, THOUGH.. ESPECIALLY IN A CREATIVE FIELD!

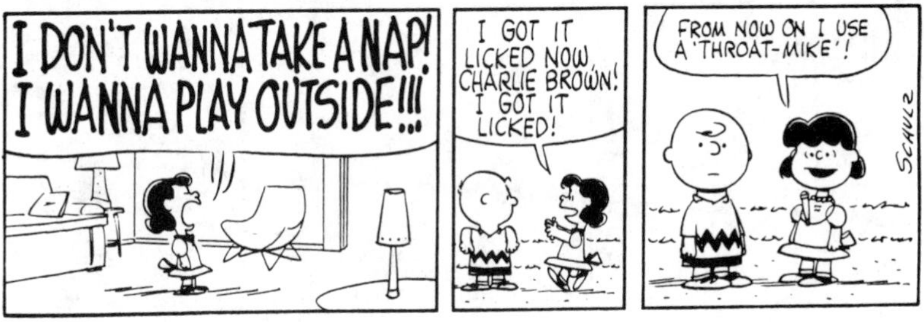
I DON'T WANNA TAKE A NAP! I WANNA PLAY OUTSIDE!!!
I GOT IT LICKED NOW, CHARLIE BROWN! I GOT IT LICKED!
FROM NOW ON I USE A 'THROAT-MIKE'!
SCHULZ

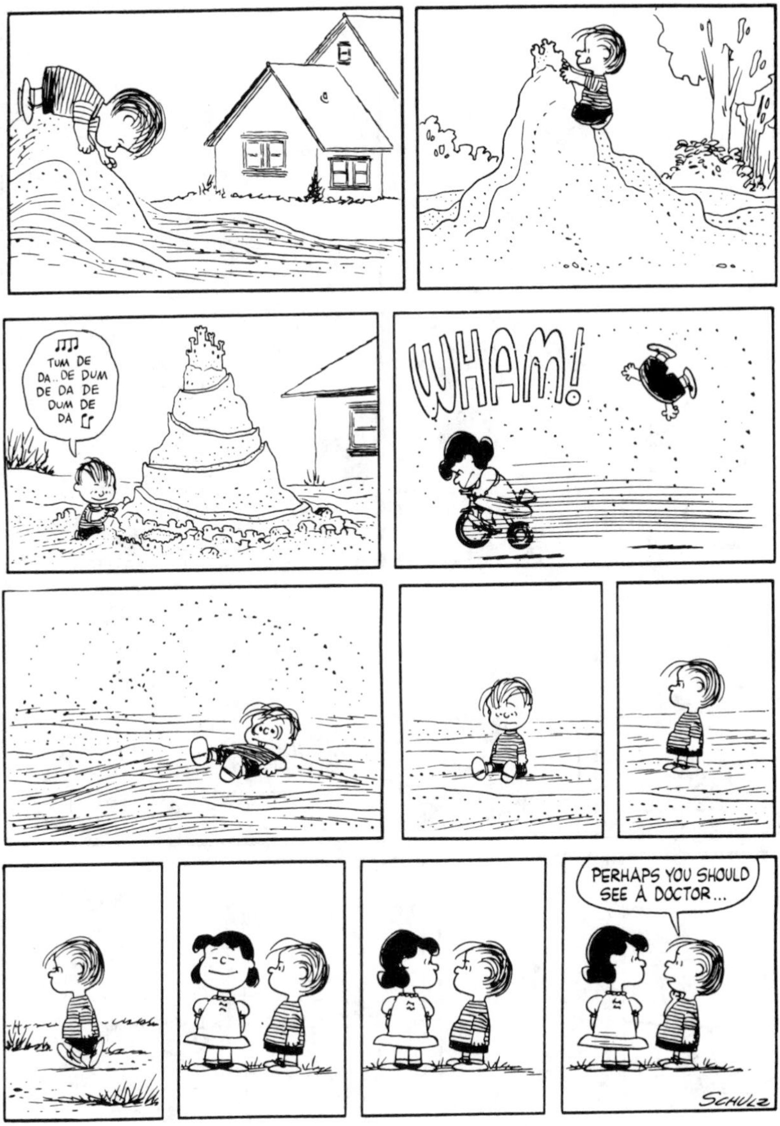

TUM DE DA.. DE DUM DE DA DE DUM DE DA
WHAM!
PERHAPS YOU SHOULD SEE A DOCTOR...
SCHULZ

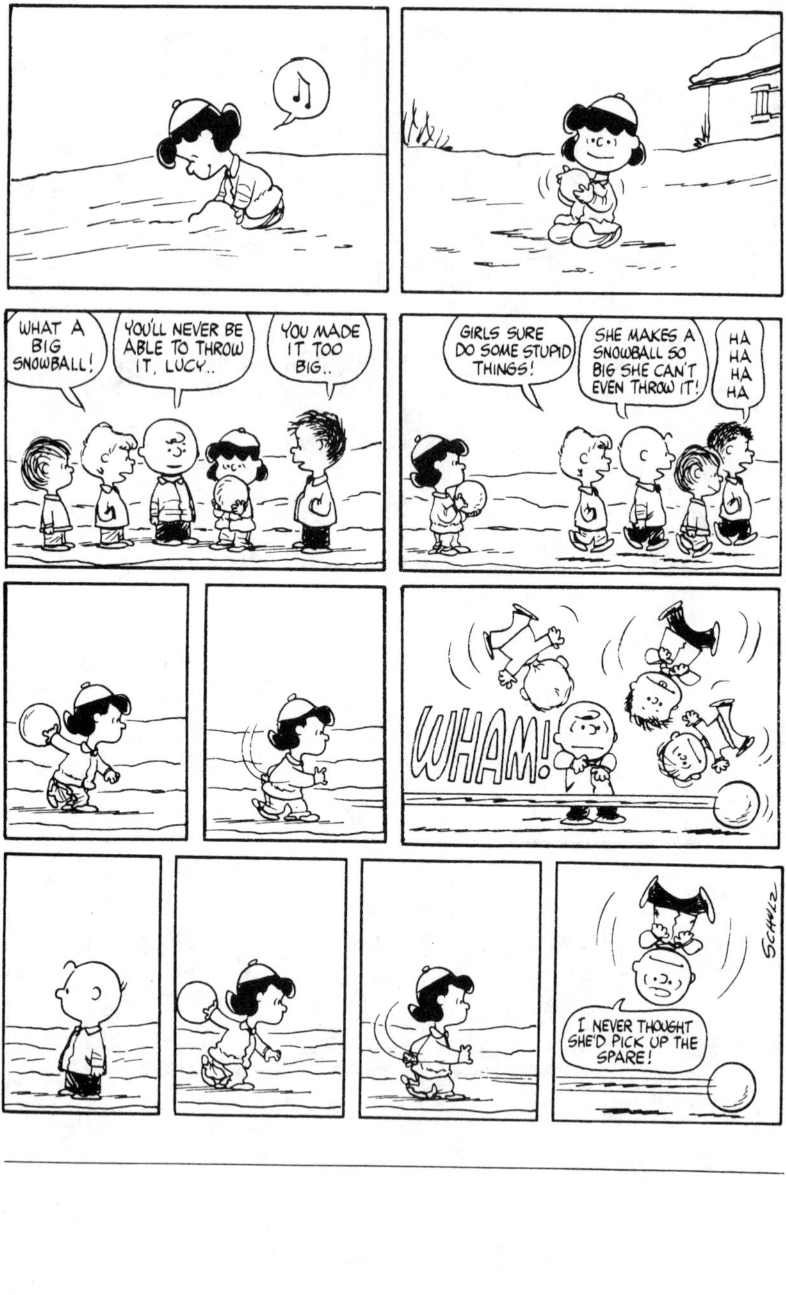
WHAT A BIG SNOWBALL!
YOU'LL NEVER BE ABLE TO THROW IT, LUCY..
YOU MADE IT TOO BIG..
GIRLS SURE DO SOME STUPID THINGS!
SHE MAKES A SNOWBALL SO BIG SHE CAN'T EVEN THROW IT!
HA HA HA HA
WHAM!
SCHULZ
I NEVER THOUGHT SHE'D PICK UP THE SPARE!

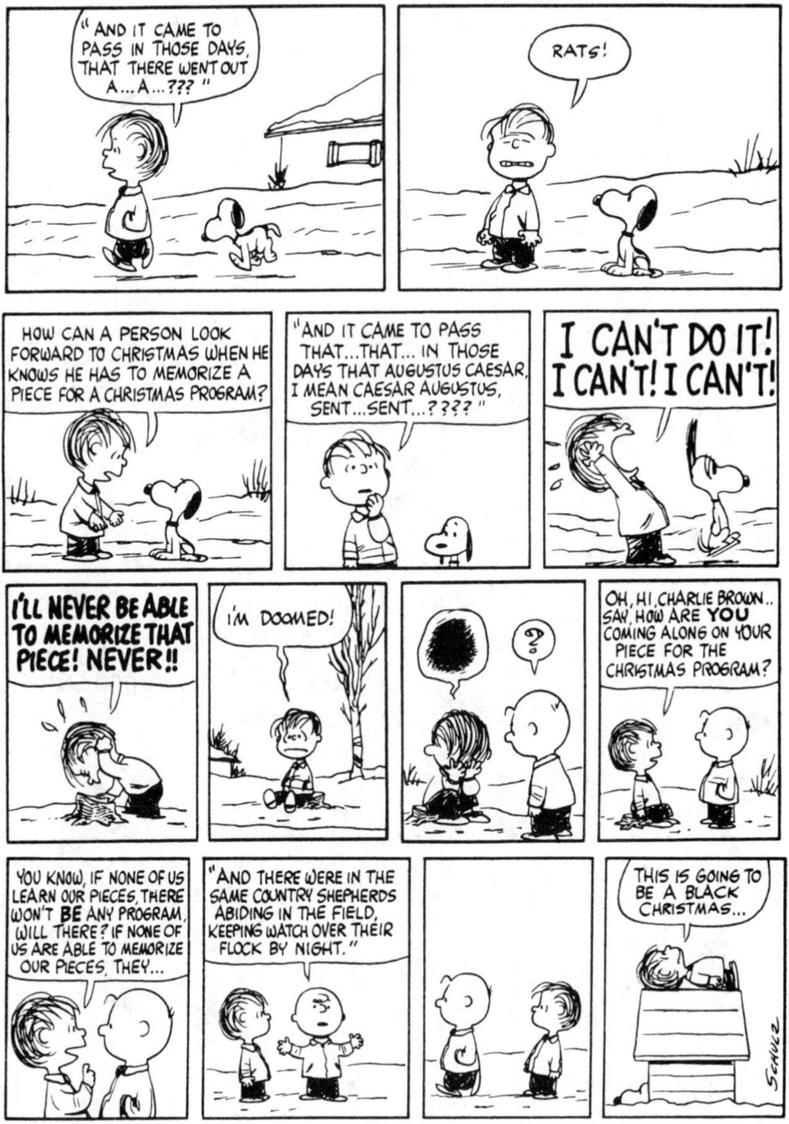
"AND IT CAME TO PASS IN THOSE DAYS, THAT THERE WENT OUT A...A...???"
RATS!
HOW CAN A PERSON LOOK FORWARD TO CHRISTMAS WHEN HE KNOWS HE HAS TO MEMORIZE A PIECE FOR A CHRISTMAS PROGRAM?
"AND IT CAME TO PASS THAT...THAT... IN THOSE DAYS THAT AUGUSTUS CAESAR, I MEAN CAESAR AUGUSTUS, SENT...SENT...????"
I CAN'T DO IT! I CAN'T! I CAN'T!
I'LL NEVER BE ABLE TO MEMORIZE THAT PIECE! NEVER!!
I'M DOOMED!
?
OH, HI, CHARLIE BROWN.. SAY, HOW ARE **YOU** COMING ALONG ON YOUR PIECE FOR THE CHRISTMAS PROGRAM?
YOU KNOW, IF NONE OF US LEARN OUR PIECES, THERE WON'T **BE** ANY PROGRAM, WILL THERE? IF NONE OF US ARE ABLE TO MEMORIZE OUR PIECES, THEY...
"AND THERE WERE IN THE SAME COUNTRY SHEPHERDS ABIDING IN THE FIELD, KEEPING WATCH OVER THEIR FLOCK BY NIGHT."
THIS IS GOING TO BE A BLACK CHRISTMAS...
SCHULZ

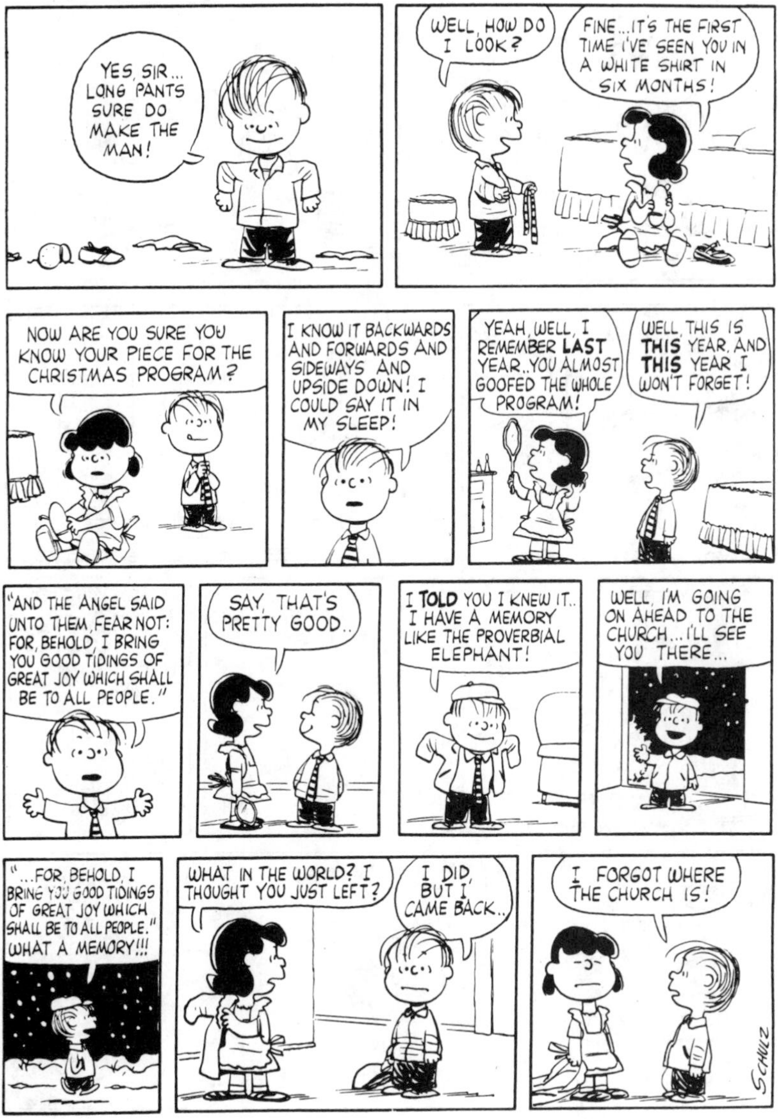
YES, SIR... LONG PANTS SURE DO MAKE THE MAN!
WELL, HOW DO I LOOK?
FINE...IT'S THE FIRST TIME I'VE SEEN YOU IN A WHITE SHIRT IN SIX MONTHS!
NOW ARE YOU SURE YOU KNOW YOUR PIECE FOR THE CHRISTMAS PROGRAM?
I KNOW IT BACKWARDS AND FORWARDS AND SIDEWAYS AND UPSIDE DOWN! I COULD SAY IT IN MY SLEEP!
YEAH, WELL, I REMEMBER LAST YEAR..YOU ALMOST GOOFED THE WHOLE PROGRAM!
WELL, THIS IS THIS YEAR, AND THIS YEAR I WON'T FORGET!
"AND THE ANGEL SAID UNTO THEM, FEAR NOT: FOR, BEHOLD, I BRING YOU GOOD TIDINGS OF GREAT JOY WHICH SHALL BE TO ALL PEOPLE."
SAY, THAT'S PRETTY GOOD..
I TOLD YOU I KNEW IT.. I HAVE A MEMORY LIKE THE PROVERBIAL ELEPHANT!
WELL, I'M GOING ON AHEAD TO THE CHURCH...I'LL SEE YOU THERE...
"...FOR, BEHOLD, I BRING YOU GOOD TIDINGS OF GREAT JOY WHICH SHALL BE TO ALL PEOPLE." WHAT A MEMORY!!!
WHAT IN THE WORLD? I THOUGHT YOU JUST LEFT?
I DID, BUT I CAME BACK..
I FORGOT WHERE THE CHURCH IS!
SCHULZ

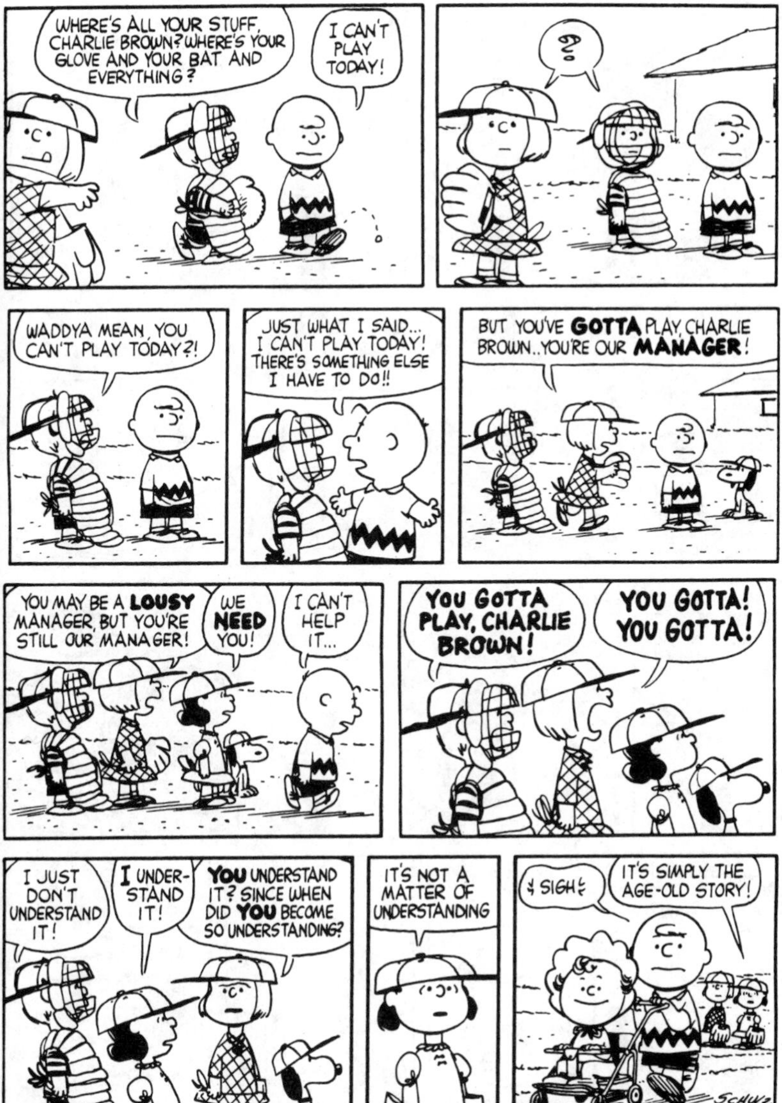
WHERE'S ALL YOUR STUFF, CHARLIE BROWN? WHERE'S YOUR GLOVE AND YOUR BAT AND EVERYTHING?
I CAN'T PLAY TODAY!
WADDYA MEAN, YOU CAN'T PLAY TODAY?!
JUST WHAT I SAID... I CAN'T PLAY TODAY! THERE'S SOMETHING ELSE I HAVE TO DO!!
BUT YOU'VE GOTTA PLAY, CHARLIE BROWN.. YOU'RE OUR MANAGER!
YOU MAY BE A LOUSY MANAGER, BUT YOU'RE STILL OUR MANAGER!
WE NEED YOU!
I CAN'T HELP IT...
YOU GOTTA PLAY, CHARLIE BROWN!
YOU GOTTA! YOU GOTTA!
I JUST DON'T UNDERSTAND IT!
I UNDER-STAND IT!
YOU UNDERSTAND IT? SINCE WHEN DID YOU BECOME SO UNDERSTANDING?
IT'S NOT A MATTER OF UNDERSTANDING
SIGH
IT'S SIMPLY THE AGE-OLD STORY!
SCHULZ

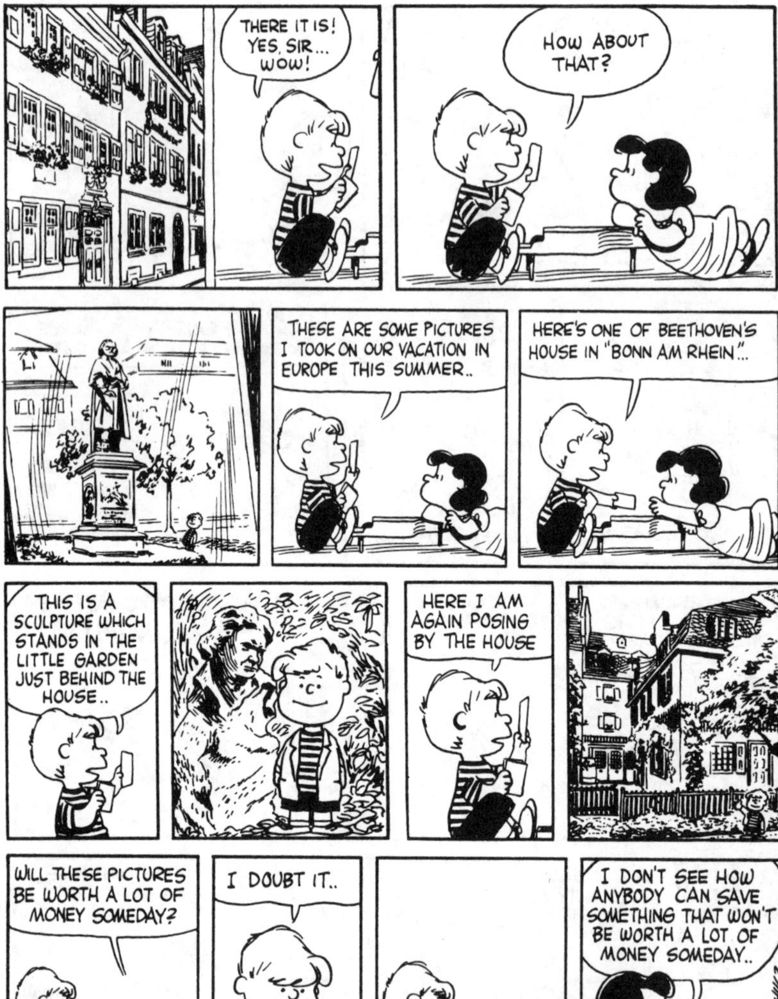
THERE IT IS! YES, SIR... WOW!
HOW ABOUT THAT?
THESE ARE SOME PICTURES I TOOK ON OUR VACATION IN EUROPE THIS SUMMER..
HERE'S ONE OF BEETHOVEN'S HOUSE IN "BONN AM RHEIN"..
THIS IS A SCULPTURE WHICH STANDS IN THE LITTLE GARDEN JUST BEHIND THE HOUSE..
HERE I AM AGAIN POSING BY THE HOUSE
WILL THESE PICTURES BE WORTH A LOT OF MONEY SOMEDAY?
I DOUBT IT..
I DON'T SEE HOW ANYBODY CAN SAVE SOMETHING THAT WON'T BE WORTH A LOT OF MONEY SOMEDAY..
SCHULZ

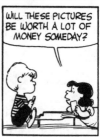

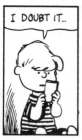

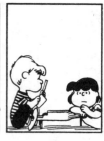

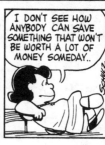

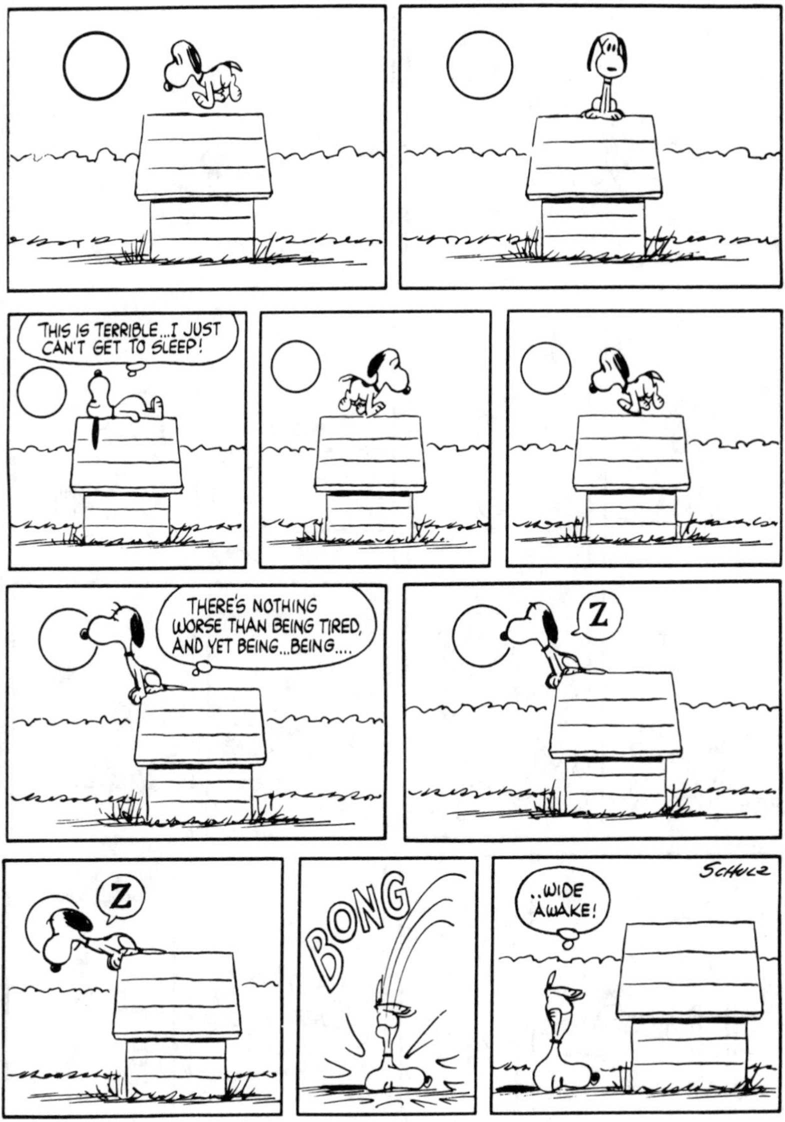
THIS IS TERRIBLE...I JUST CAN'T GET TO SLEEP!
THERE'S NOTHING WORSE THAN BEING TIRED, AND YET BEING...BEING....
Z
Z
BONG
..WIDE AWAKE!
SCHULZ

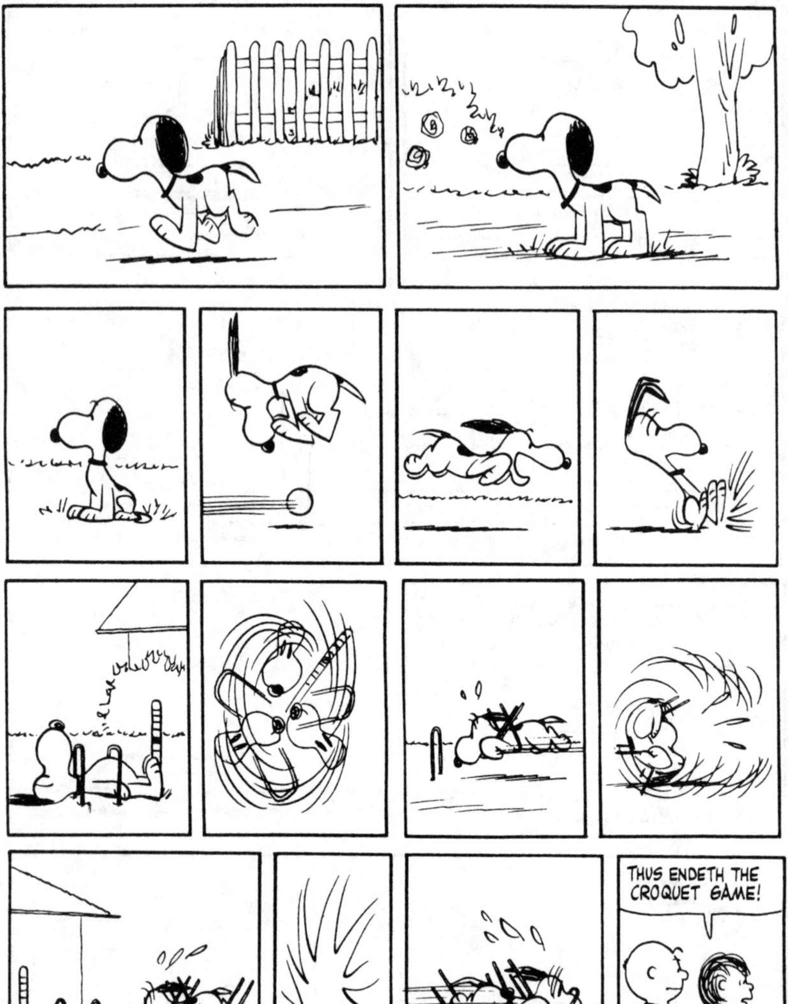
THUS ENDETH THE CROQUET GAME!
SCHULZ

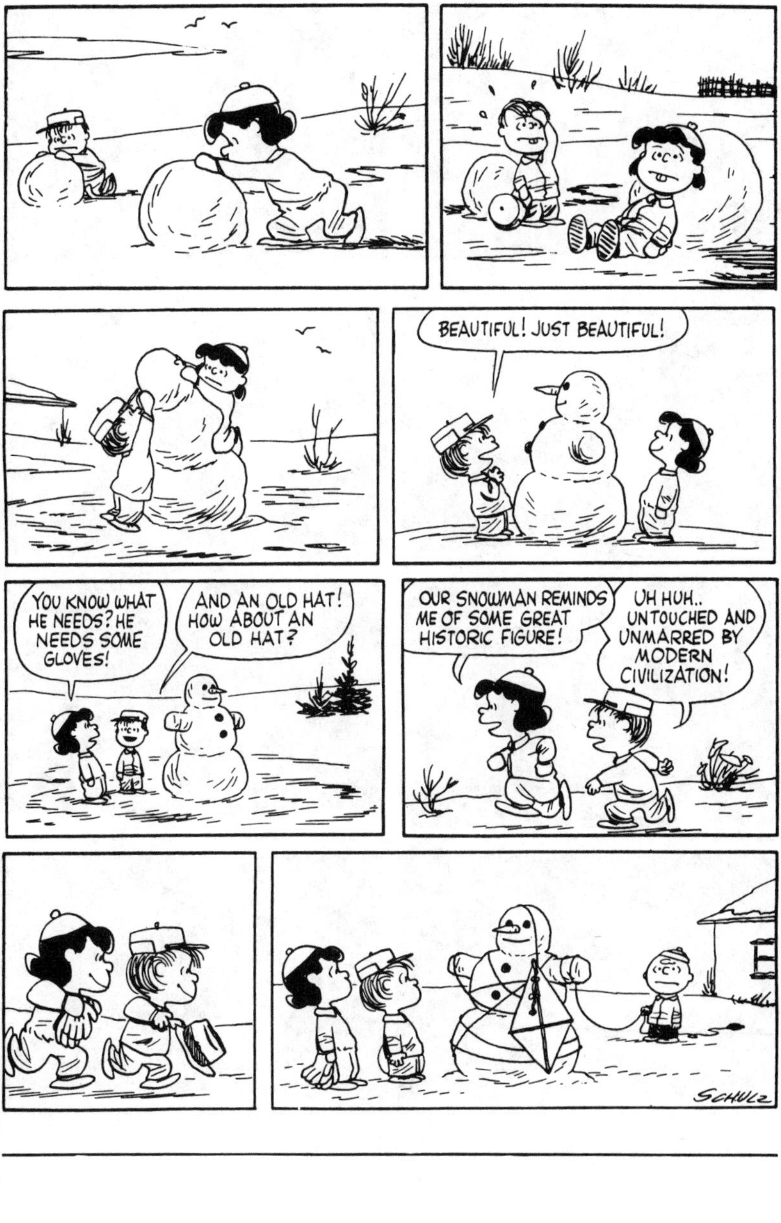
BEAUTIFUL! JUST BEAUTIFUL!
YOU KNOW WHAT HE NEEDS? HE NEEDS SOME GLOVES!
AND AN OLD HAT! HOW ABOUT AN OLD HAT?
OUR SNOWMAN REMINDS ME OF SOME GREAT HISTORIC FIGURE!
UH HUH.. UNTOUCHED AND UNMARRED BY MODERN CIVILIZATION!
SCHULZ

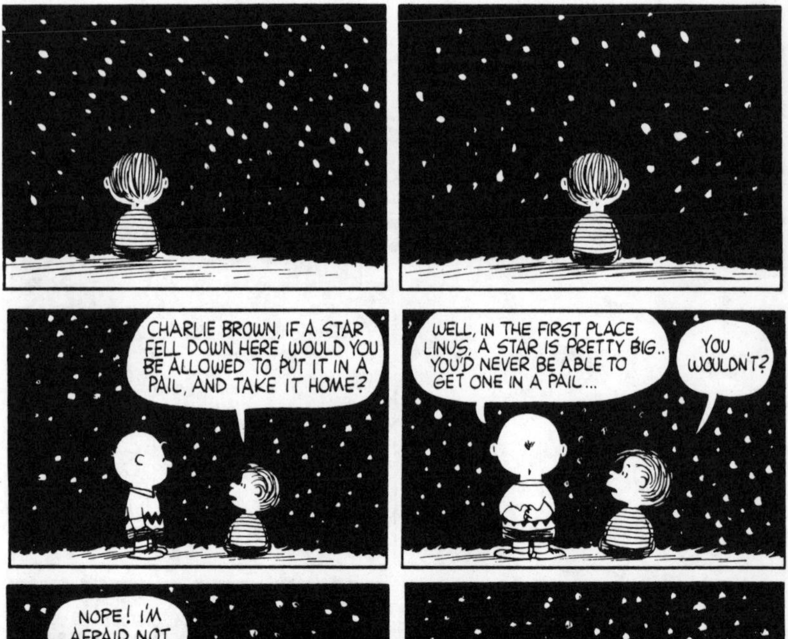
CHARLIE BROWN, IF A STAR FELL DOWN HERE, WOULD YOU BE ALLOWED TO PUT IT IN A PAIL, AND TAKE IT HOME?
WELL, IN THE FIRST PLACE LINUS, A STAR IS PRETTY BIG.. YOU'D NEVER BE ABLE TO GET ONE IN A PAIL...
YOU WOULDN'T?
NOPE! I'M AFRAID NOT..
SCHULZ

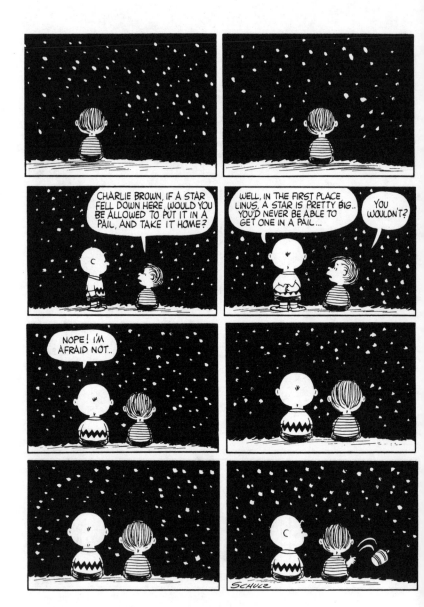

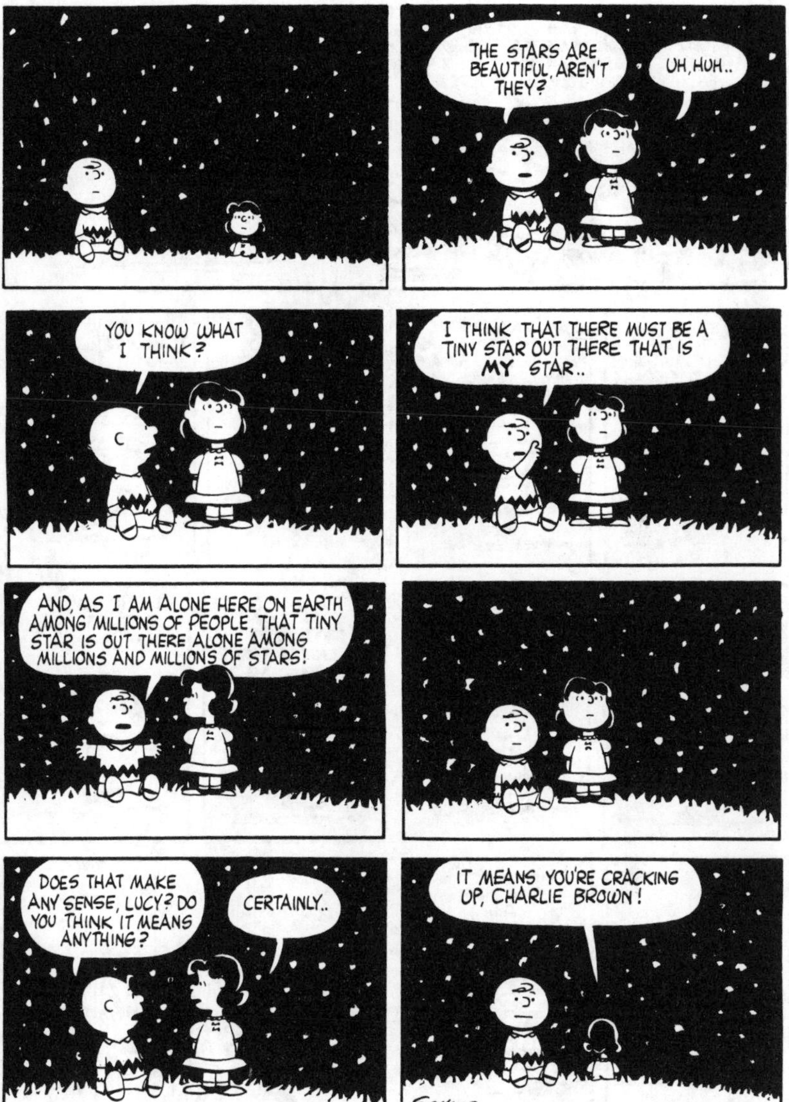

THE STARS ARE BEAUTIFUL, AREN'T THEY?
UH, HUH..
YOU KNOW WHAT I THINK?
I THINK THAT THERE MUST BE A TINY STAR OUT THERE THAT IS MY STAR..
AND, AS I AM ALONE HERE ON EARTH AMONG MILLIONS OF PEOPLE, THAT TINY STAR IS OUT THERE ALONE AMONG MILLIONS AND MILLIONS OF STARS!
DOES THAT MAKE ANY SENSE, LUCY? DO YOU THINK IT MEANS ANYTHING?
CERTAINLY..
IT MEANS YOU'RE CRACKING UP, CHARLIE BROWN!
SCHULZ

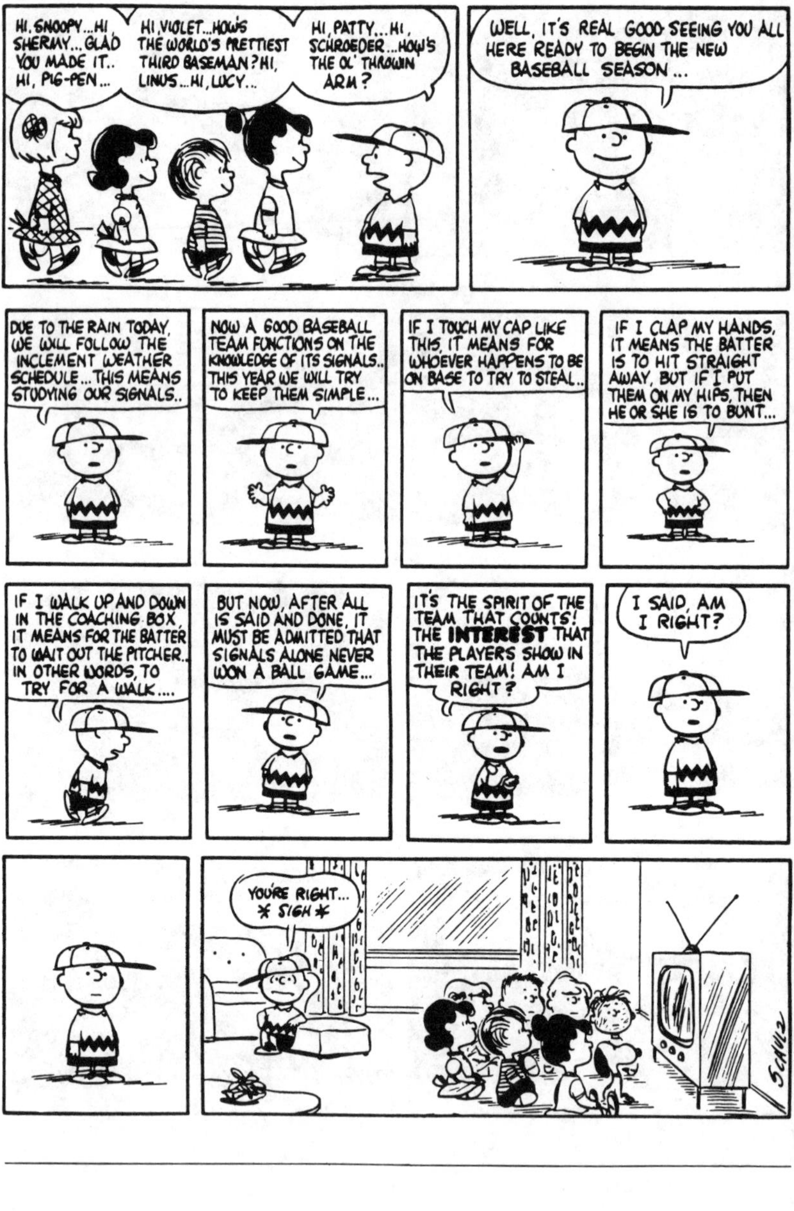
HI, SNOOPY...HI, SHERMY...GLAD YOU MADE IT.. HI, PIG-PEN...
HI, VIOLET...HOW'S THE WORLD'S PRETTIEST THIRD BASEMAN? HI, LINUS...HI, LUCY...
HI, PATTY...HI, SCHROEDER...HOW'S THE OL' THROWIN ARM?
WELL, IT'S REAL GOOD SEEING YOU ALL HERE READY TO BEGIN THE NEW BASEBALL SEASON...
DUE TO THE RAIN TODAY, WE WILL FOLLOW THE INCLEMENT WEATHER SCHEDULE...THIS MEANS STUDYING OUR SIGNALS..
NOW A GOOD BASEBALL TEAM FUNCTIONS ON THE KNOWLEDGE OF ITS SIGNALS.. THIS YEAR WE WILL TRY TO KEEP THEM SIMPLE...
IF I TOUCH MY CAP LIKE THIS, IT MEANS FOR WHOEVER HAPPENS TO BE ON BASE TO TRY TO STEAL..
IF I CLAP MY HANDS, IT MEANS THE BATTER IS TO HIT STRAIGHT AWAY, BUT IF I PUT THEM ON MY HIPS, THEN HE OR SHE IS TO BUNT...
IF I WALK UP AND DOWN IN THE COACHING BOX, IT MEANS FOR THE BATTER TO WAIT OUT THE PITCHER.. IN OTHER WORDS, TO TRY FOR A WALK....
BUT NOW, AFTER ALL IS SAID AND DONE, IT MUST BE ADMITTED THAT SIGNALS ALONE NEVER WON A BALL GAME...
IT'S THE SPIRIT OF THE TEAM THAT COUNTS! THE INTEREST THAT THE PLAYERS SHOW IN THEIR TEAM! AM I RIGHT?
I SAID, AM I RIGHT?
YOU'RE RIGHT... * SIGH *
SCHULZ

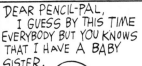

DEAR PENCIL-PAL,
I GUESS BY THIS TIME EVERYBODY BUT YOU KNOWS THAT I HAVE A BABY SISTER.

I SHOULD HAVE WRITTEN SOONER TO TELL YOU, BUT I HAVE BEEN VERY BUSY. HER NAME IS SALLY. WE LIKE HER AND SHE LIKES US.

OH, OH!

IN A WAY, THIS HAS BEEN A GOOD EXPERIENCE FOR ME. I HAVE LEARNED A LOT.
AS EVER,
CHARLIE BROWN

SCHULZ

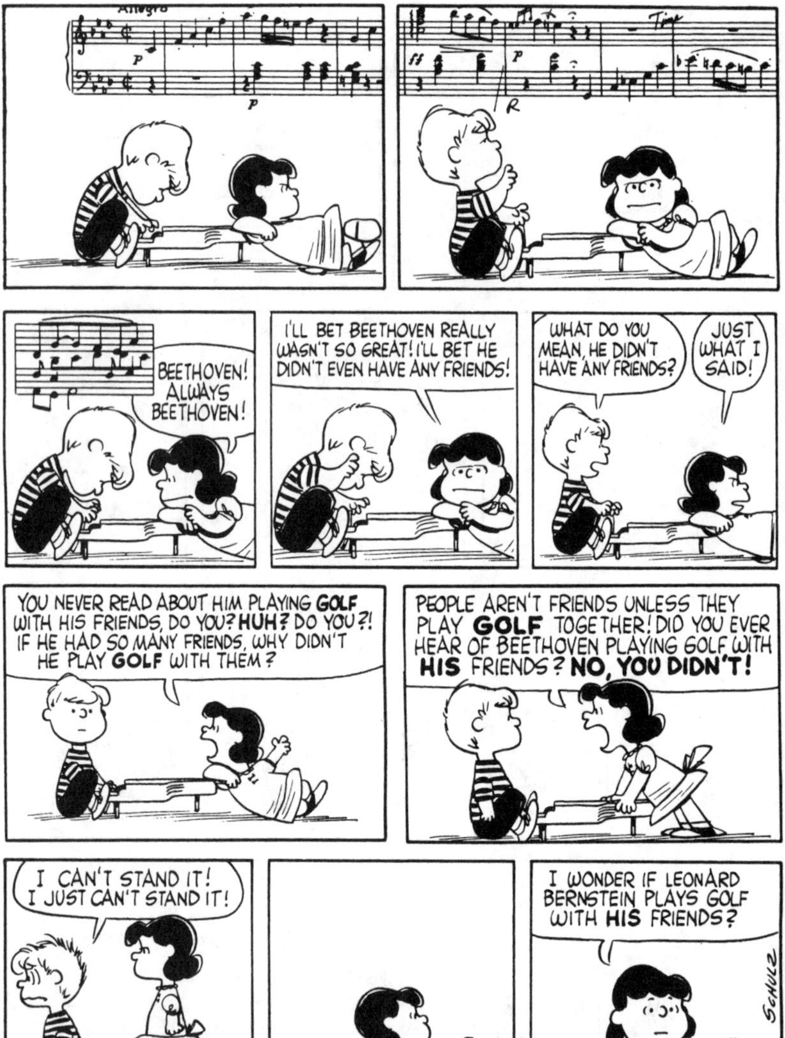
BEETHOVEN! ALWAYS BEETHOVEN!
I'LL BET BEETHOVEN REALLY WASN'T SO GREAT! I'LL BET HE DIDN'T EVEN HAVE ANY FRIENDS!
WHAT DO YOU MEAN, HE DIDN'T HAVE ANY FRIENDS?
JUST WHAT I SAID!
YOU NEVER READ ABOUT HIM PLAYING GOLF WITH HIS FRIENDS, DO YOU? HUH? DO YOU?! IF HE HAD SO MANY FRIENDS, WHY DIDN'T HE PLAY GOLF WITH THEM?
PEOPLE AREN'T FRIENDS UNLESS THEY PLAY GOLF TOGETHER! DID YOU EVER HEAR OF BEETHOVEN PLAYING GOLF WITH HIS FRIENDS? NO, YOU DIDN'T!
I CAN'T STAND IT! I JUST CAN'T STAND IT!
I WONDER IF LEONARD BERNSTEIN PLAYS GOLF WITH HIS FRIENDS?
SCHULZ

CLOMP!

WHAM

WEAK ANKLES!

SCHULZ

READY?
READY!
..TAKE A DEEP BREATH...
NOW HOLD IT!
WOOOSH!
WOOSH!!
SCHULZ

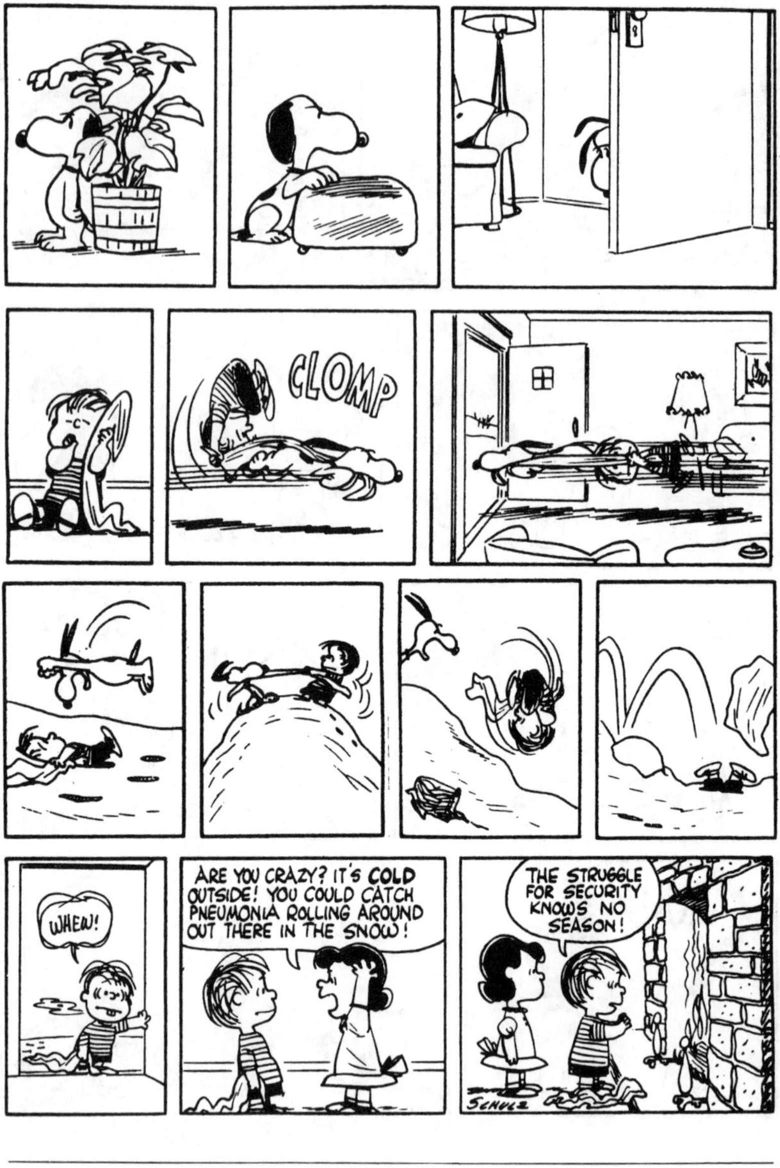
CLOMP
WHEW!
ARE YOU CRAZY? IT'S COLD OUTSIDE! YOU COULD CATCH PNEUMONIA ROLLING AROUND OUT THERE IN THE SNOW!
THE STRUGGLE FOR SECURITY KNOWS NO SEASON!
SCHULZ

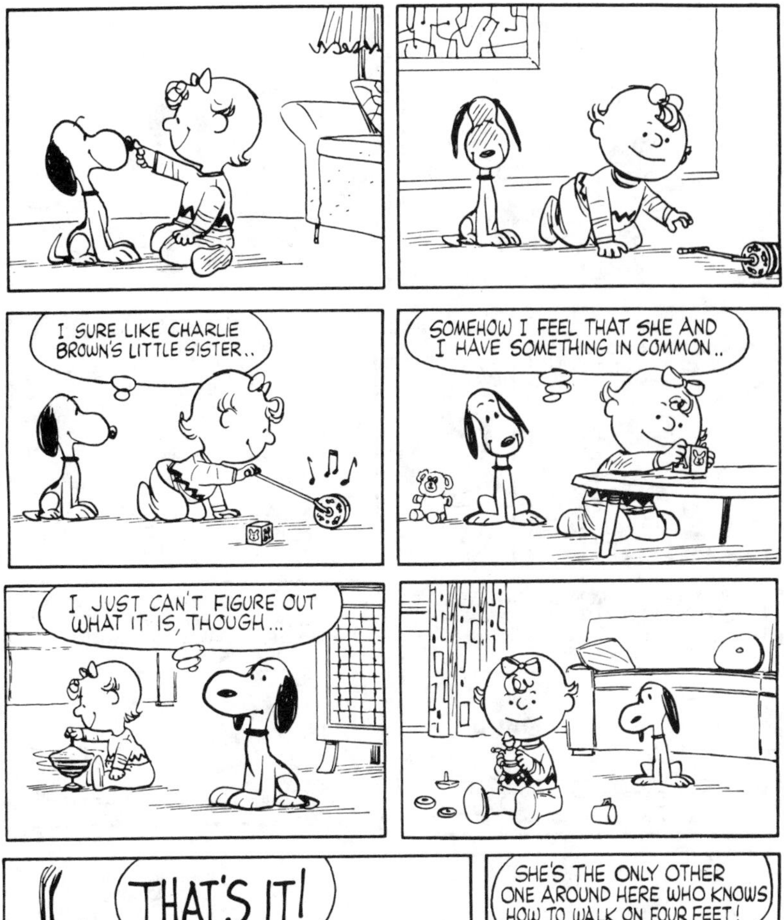
I SURE LIKE CHARLIE BROWN'S LITTLE SISTER..
SOMEHOW I FEEL THAT SHE AND I HAVE SOMETHING IN COMMON..
I JUST CAN'T FIGURE OUT WHAT IT IS, THOUGH...
THAT'S IT!
SHE'S THE ONLY OTHER ONE AROUND HERE WHO KNOWS HOW TO WALK ON FOUR FEET!
SCHULZ

"THE FIRST MATE IS CALLING, SIR...YOU'RE WANTED ON DECK!"
"AH, ME... IS THERE NO REST FOR THE WEARY?"
IT'S A STORMY NIGHT AT SEA..
THE CAPTAIN REALIZES HIS SHIP IS IN TROUBLE.. THE CREW IS FRIGHTENED..
THE STORM RAGES AS THE HUNDRED-FOOT WAVES SMASH AGAINST THE SHIP!
WHAT AN INSPIRATION IT IS TO THE MEN TO SEE THEIR CAPTAIN STANDING BRAVELY ON THE BRIDGE!
ABANDON SHIP!!
WISE GUY!
SCHULZ

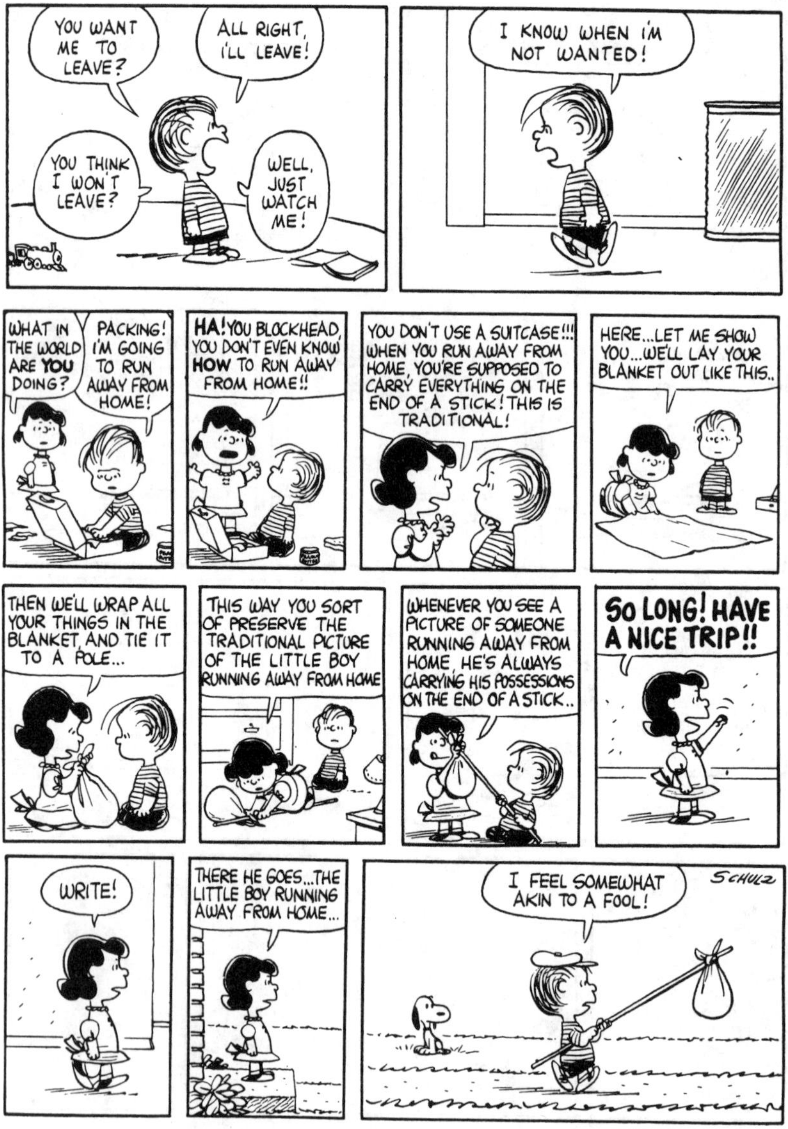
YOU WANT ME TO LEAVE?
ALL RIGHT, I'LL LEAVE!
YOU THINK I WON'T LEAVE?
WELL, JUST WATCH ME!
I KNOW WHEN I'M NOT WANTED!
WHAT IN THE WORLD ARE **YOU** DOING?
PACKING! I'M GOING TO RUN AWAY FROM HOME!
**HA!** YOU BLOCKHEAD, YOU DON'T EVEN KNOW **HOW** TO RUN AWAY FROM HOME!!
YOU DON'T USE A SUITCASE!!! WHEN YOU RUN AWAY FROM HOME, YOU'RE SUPPOSED TO CARRY EVERYTHING ON THE END OF A STICK! THIS IS TRADITIONAL!
HERE...LET ME SHOW YOU...WE'LL LAY YOUR BLANKET OUT LIKE THIS..
THEN WE'LL WRAP ALL YOUR THINGS IN THE BLANKET, AND TIE IT TO A POLE...
THIS WAY YOU SORT OF PRESERVE THE TRADITIONAL PICTURE OF THE LITTLE BOY RUNNING AWAY FROM HOME
WHENEVER YOU SEE A PICTURE OF SOMEONE RUNNING AWAY FROM HOME, HE'S ALWAYS CARRYING HIS POSSESSIONS ON THE END OF A STICK..
SO LONG! HAVE A NICE TRIP!!
WRITE!
THERE HE GOES...THE LITTLE BOY RUNNING AWAY FROM HOME...
I FEEL SOMEWHAT AKIN TO A FOOL!
SCHULZ

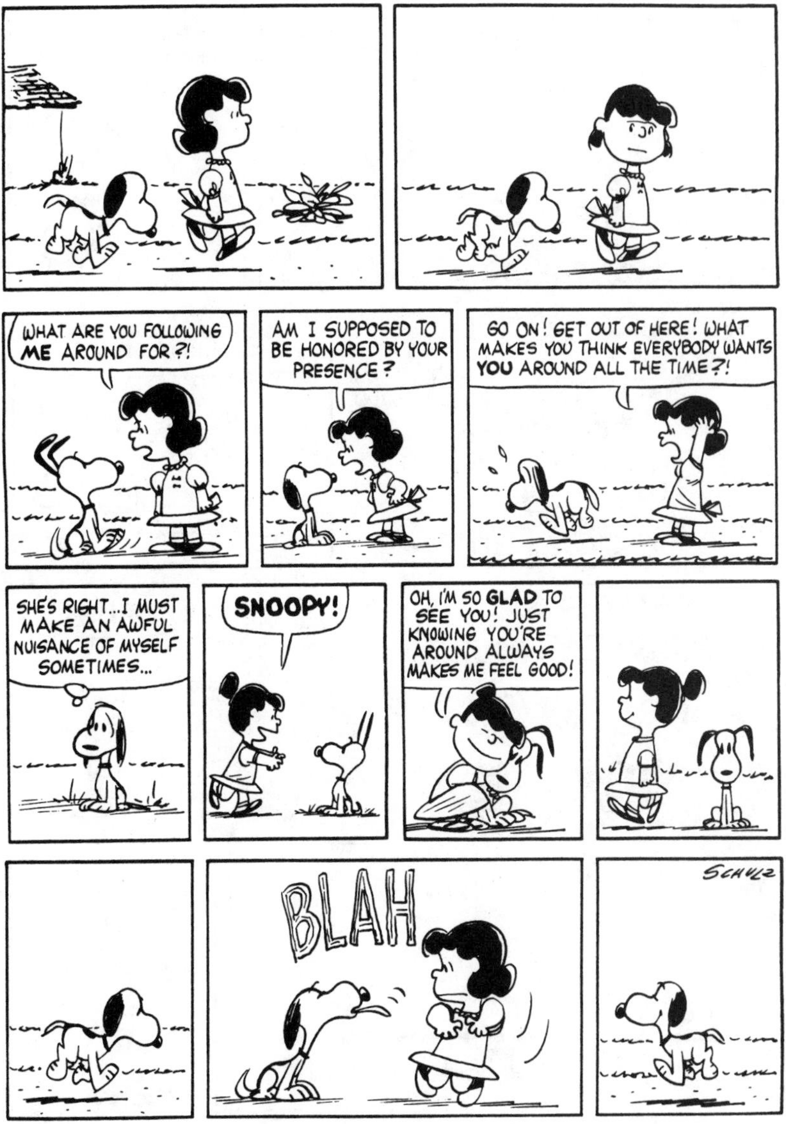
WHAT ARE YOU FOLLOWING ME AROUND FOR ?!
AM I SUPPOSED TO BE HONORED BY YOUR PRESENCE ?
GO ON! GET OUT OF HERE! WHAT MAKES YOU THINK EVERYBODY WANTS YOU AROUND ALL THE TIME ?!
SHE'S RIGHT...I MUST MAKE AN AWFUL NUISANCE OF MYSELF SOMETIMES...
SNOOPY!
OH, I'M SO GLAD TO SEE YOU! JUST KNOWING YOU'RE AROUND ALWAYS MAKES ME FEEL GOOD!
BLAH
SCHULZ

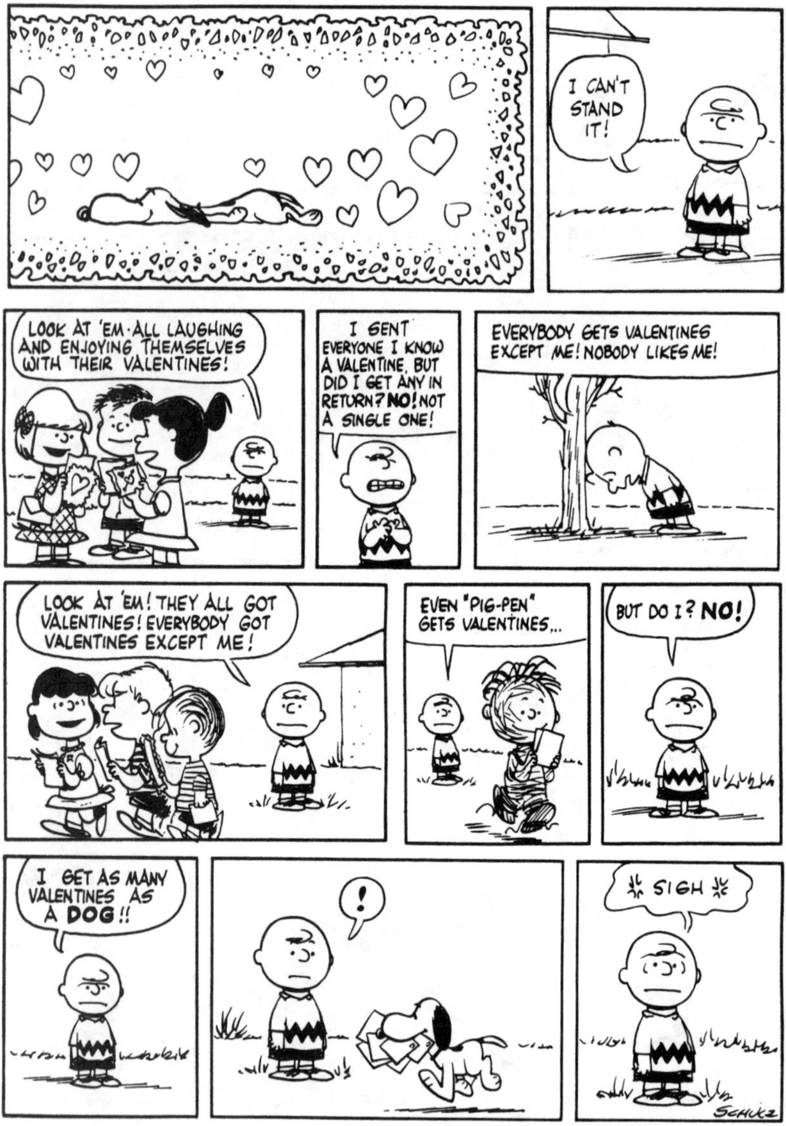
I CAN'T STAND IT!
LOOK AT 'EM ALL LAUGHING AND ENJOYING THEMSELVES WITH THEIR VALENTINES!
I SENT EVERYONE I KNOW A VALENTINE, BUT DID I GET ANY IN RETURN? NO! NOT A SINGLE ONE!
EVERYBODY GETS VALENTINES EXCEPT ME! NOBODY LIKES ME!
LOOK AT 'EM! THEY ALL GOT VALENTINES! EVERYBODY GOT VALENTINES EXCEPT ME!
EVEN "PIG-PEN" GETS VALENTINES...
BUT DO I? NO!
I GET AS MANY VALENTINES AS A DOG!!
!
SIGH
SCHULZ

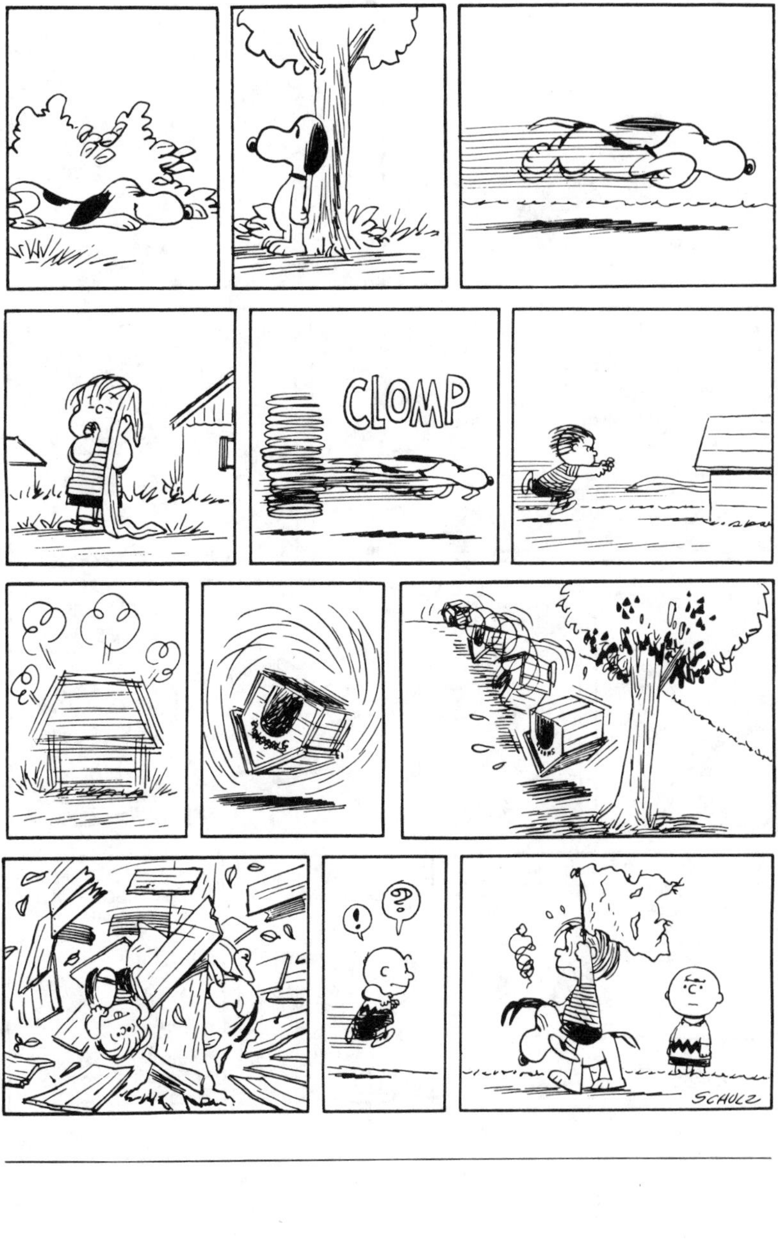
CLOMP
SCHULZ

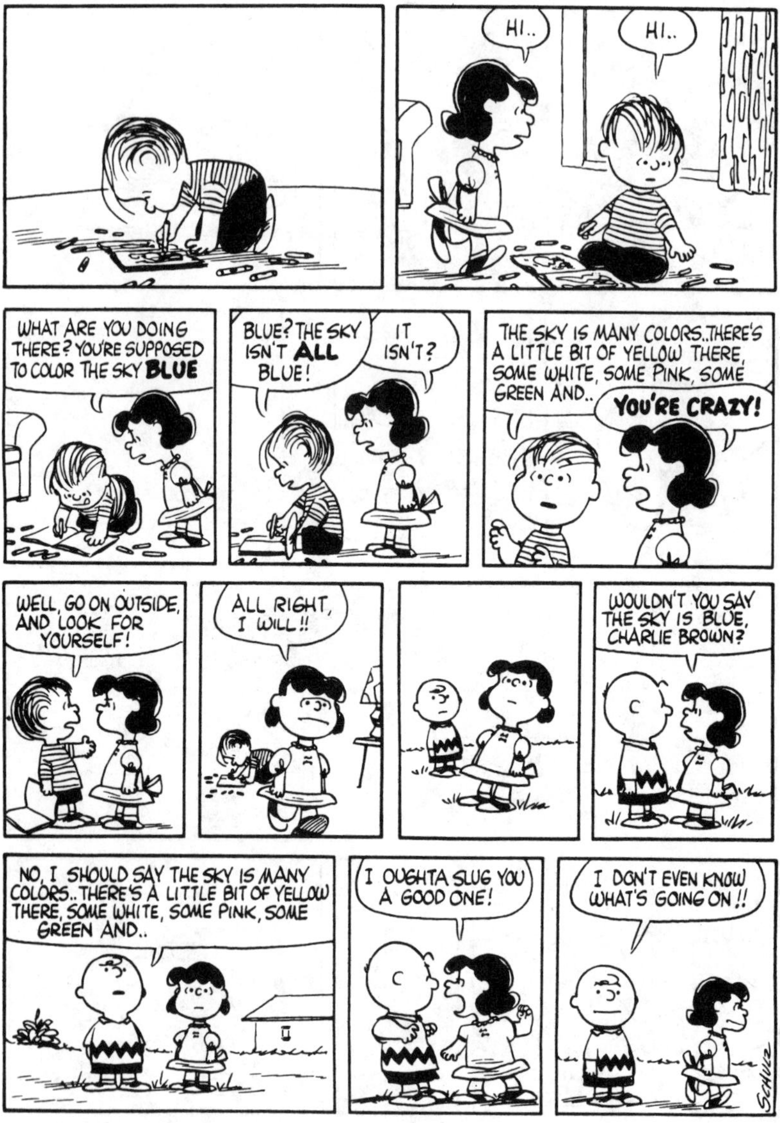
HI..
HI..
WHAT ARE YOU DOING THERE? YOU'RE SUPPOSED TO COLOR THE SKY BLUE
BLUE? THE SKY ISN'T ALL BLUE!
IT ISN'T?
THE SKY IS MANY COLORS..THERE'S A LITTLE BIT OF YELLOW THERE, SOME WHITE, SOME PINK, SOME GREEN AND..
YOU'RE CRAZY!
WELL, GO ON OUTSIDE, AND LOOK FOR YOURSELF!
ALL RIGHT, I WILL!!
WOULDN'T YOU SAY THE SKY IS BLUE, CHARLIE BROWN?
NO, I SHOULD SAY THE SKY IS MANY COLORS..THERE'S A LITTLE BIT OF YELLOW THERE, SOME WHITE, SOME PINK, SOME GREEN AND..
I OUGHTA SLUG YOU A GOOD ONE!
I DON'T EVEN KNOW WHAT'S GOING ON!!
SCHULZ

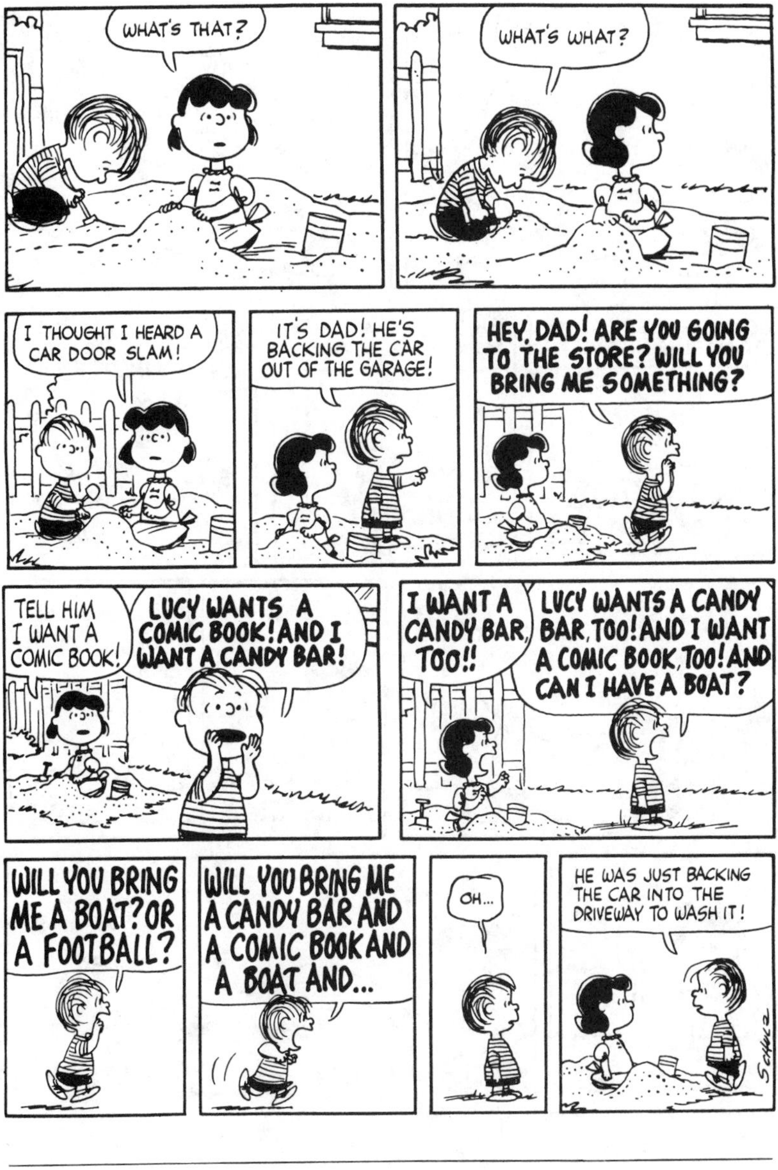
WHAT'S THAT?
WHAT'S WHAT?
I THOUGHT I HEARD A CAR DOOR SLAM!
IT'S DAD! HE'S BACKING THE CAR OUT OF THE GARAGE!
HEY, DAD! ARE YOU GOING TO THE STORE? WILL YOU BRING ME SOMETHING?
TELL HIM I WANT A COMIC BOOK!
LUCY WANTS A COMIC BOOK! AND I WANT A CANDY BAR!
I WANT A CANDY BAR, TOO!!
LUCY WANTS A CANDY BAR, TOO! AND I WANT A COMIC BOOK, TOO! AND CAN I HAVE A BOAT?
WILL YOU BRING ME A BOAT? OR A FOOTBALL?
WILL YOU BRING ME A CANDY BAR AND A COMIC BOOK AND A BOAT AND...
OH...
HE WAS JUST BACKING THE CAR INTO THE DRIVEWAY TO WASH IT!
SCHULZ

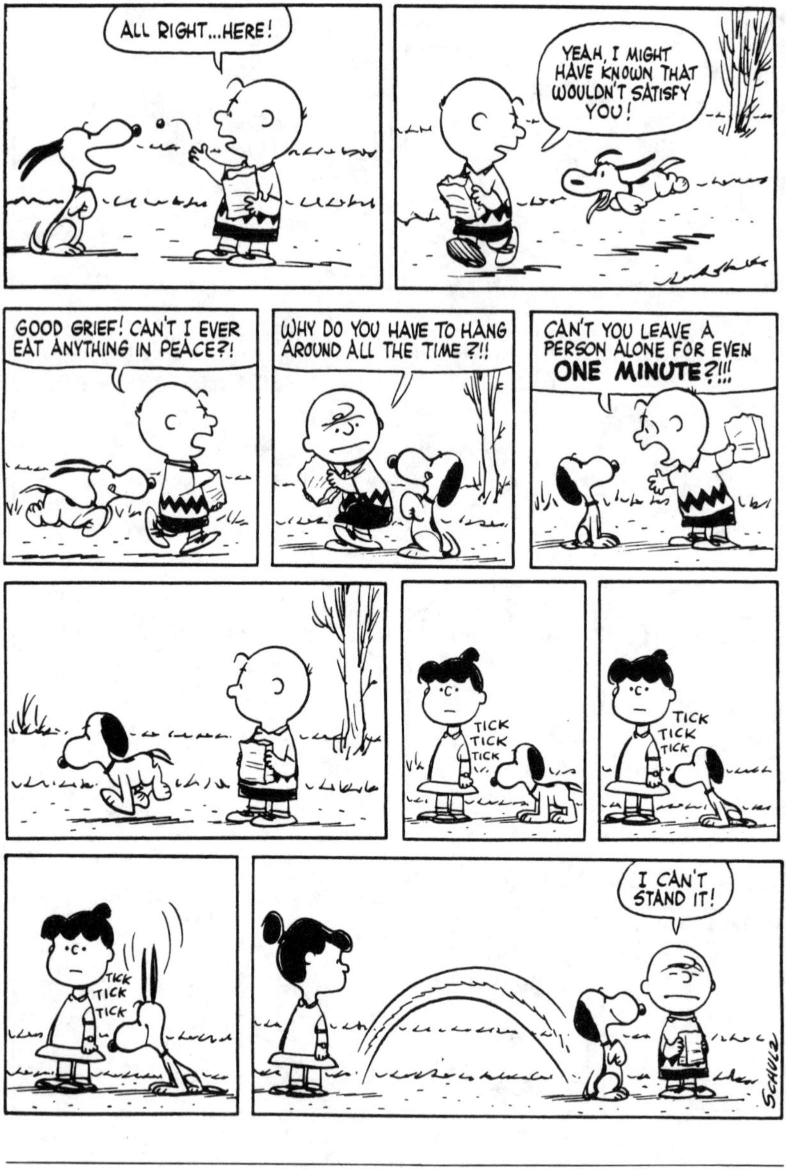
ALL RIGHT...HERE!
YEAH, I MIGHT HAVE KNOWN THAT WOULDN'T SATISFY YOU!
GOOD GRIEF! CAN'T I EVER EAT ANYTHING IN PEACE?!
WHY DO YOU HAVE TO HANG AROUND ALL THE TIME?!!
CAN'T YOU LEAVE A PERSON ALONE FOR EVEN ONE MINUTE?!!!
TICK TICK TICK
TICK TICK TICK
TICK TICK TICK
I CAN'T STAND IT!
SCHULZ

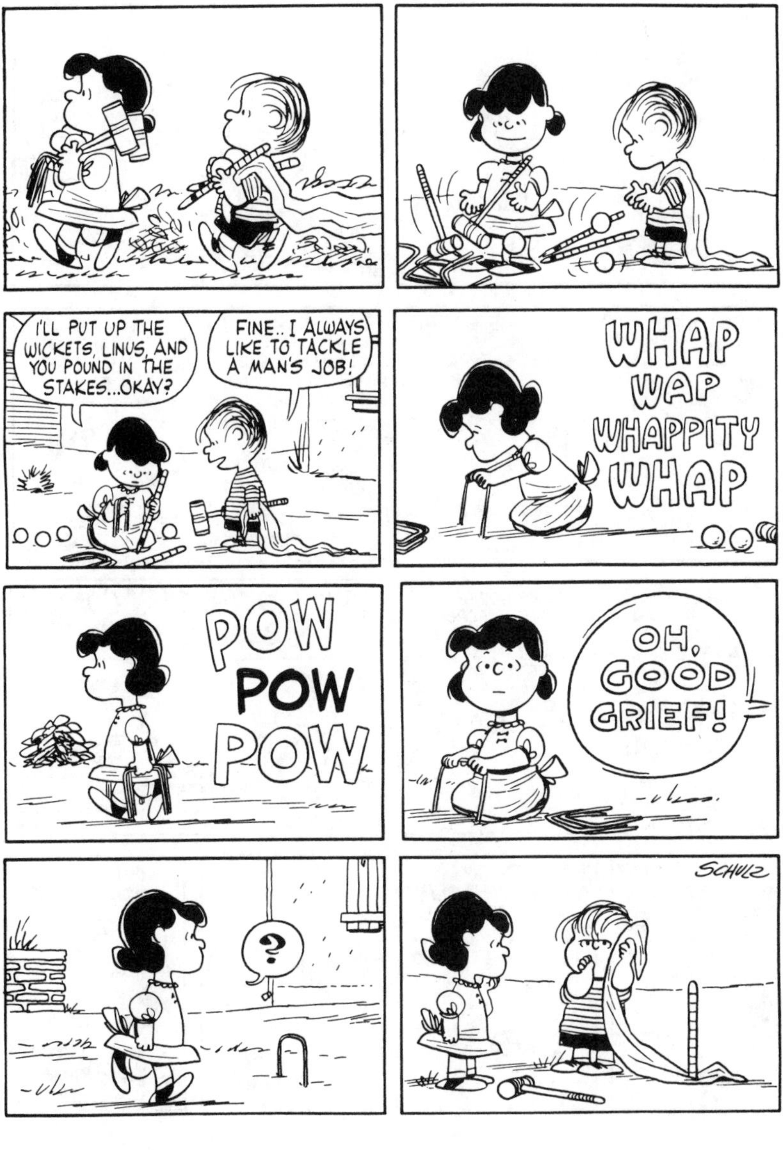
I'LL PUT UP THE WICKETS, LINUS, AND YOU POUND IN THE STAKES...OKAY?
FINE.. I ALWAYS LIKE TO TACKLE A MAN'S JOB!
WHAP
WAP
WHAPPITY
WHAP
POW
POW
POW
OH, GOOD GRIEF!
?
SCHULZ

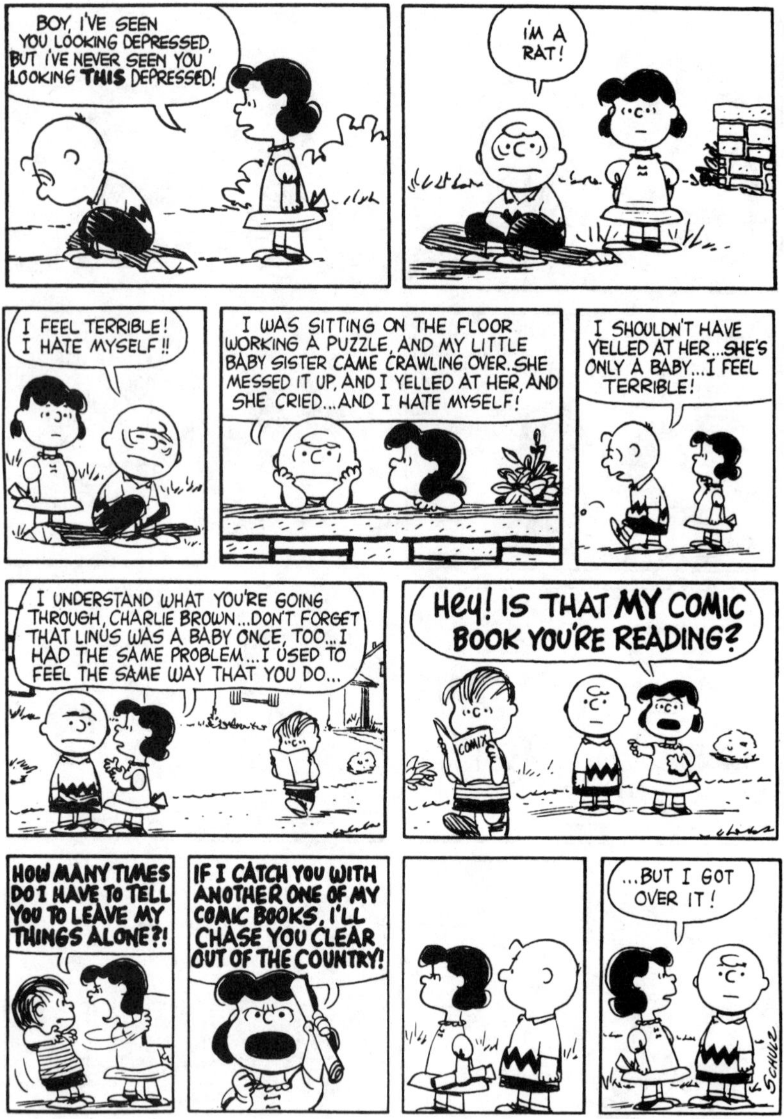
BOY, I'VE SEEN YOU LOOKING DEPRESSED, BUT I'VE NEVER SEEN YOU LOOKING THIS DEPRESSED!
I'M A RAT!
I FEEL TERRIBLE! I HATE MYSELF!!
I WAS SITTING ON THE FLOOR WORKING A PUZZLE, AND MY LITTLE BABY SISTER CAME CRAWLING OVER. SHE MESSED IT UP, AND I YELLED AT HER, AND SHE CRIED...AND I HATE MYSELF!
I SHOULDN'T HAVE YELLED AT HER...SHE'S ONLY A BABY...I FEEL TERRIBLE!
I UNDERSTAND WHAT YOU'RE GOING THROUGH, CHARLIE BROWN...DON'T FORGET THAT LINUS WAS A BABY ONCE, TOO...I HAD THE SAME PROBLEM...I USED TO FEEL THE SAME WAY THAT YOU DO...
Hey! IS THAT MY COMIC BOOK YOU'RE READING?
COMIX
HOW MANY TIMES DO I HAVE TO TELL YOU TO LEAVE MY THINGS ALONE?!
IF I CATCH YOU WITH ANOTHER ONE OF MY COMIC BOOKS, I'LL CHASE YOU CLEAR OUT OF THE COUNTRY!
...BUT I GOT OVER IT!
SCHULZ

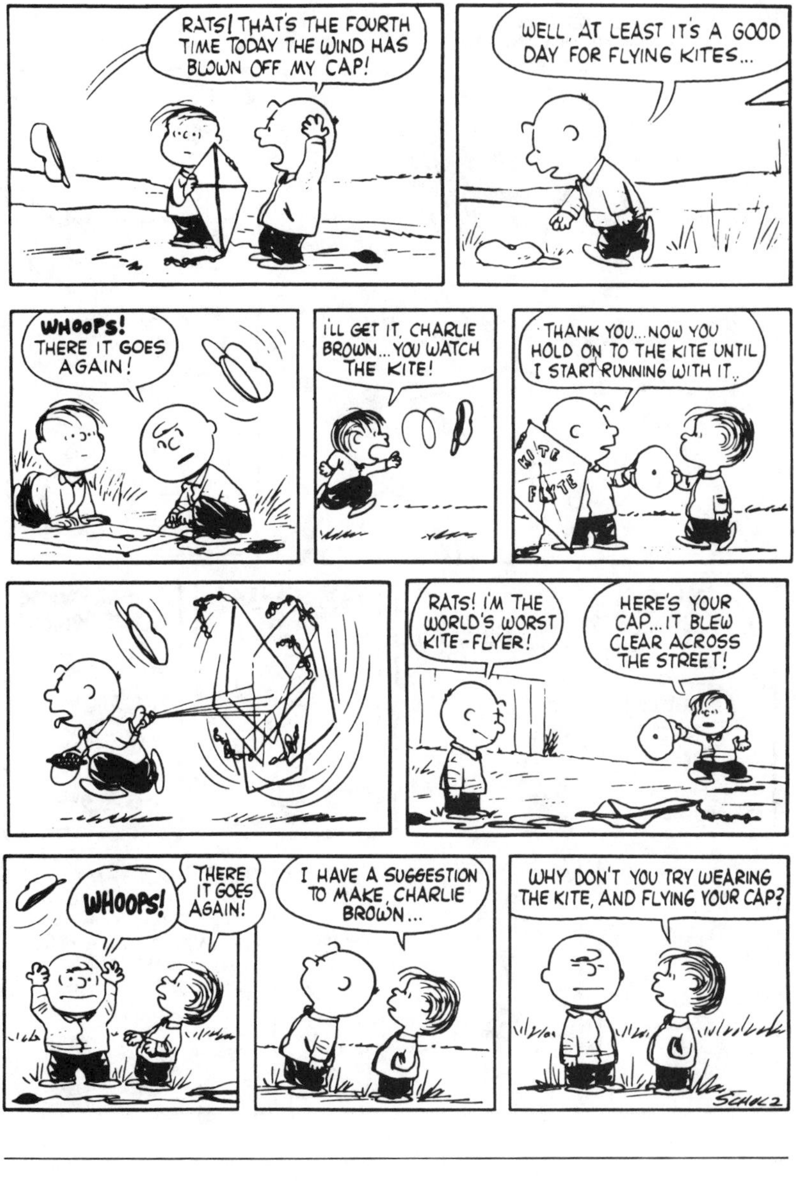
RATS! THAT'S THE FOURTH TIME TODAY THE WIND HAS BLOWN OFF MY CAP!
WELL, AT LEAST IT'S A GOOD DAY FOR FLYING KITES...
WHOOPS! THERE IT GOES AGAIN!
I'LL GET IT, CHARLIE BROWN... YOU WATCH THE KITE!
THANK YOU... NOW YOU HOLD ON TO THE KITE UNTIL I START RUNNING WITH IT..
KITE
FLYTE
RATS! I'M THE WORLD'S WORST KITE-FLYER!
HERE'S YOUR CAP... IT BLEW CLEAR ACROSS THE STREET!
WHOOPS!
THERE IT GOES AGAIN!
I HAVE A SUGGESTION TO MAKE, CHARLIE BROWN...
WHY DON'T YOU TRY WEARING THE KITE, AND FLYING YOUR CAP?
SCHULZ

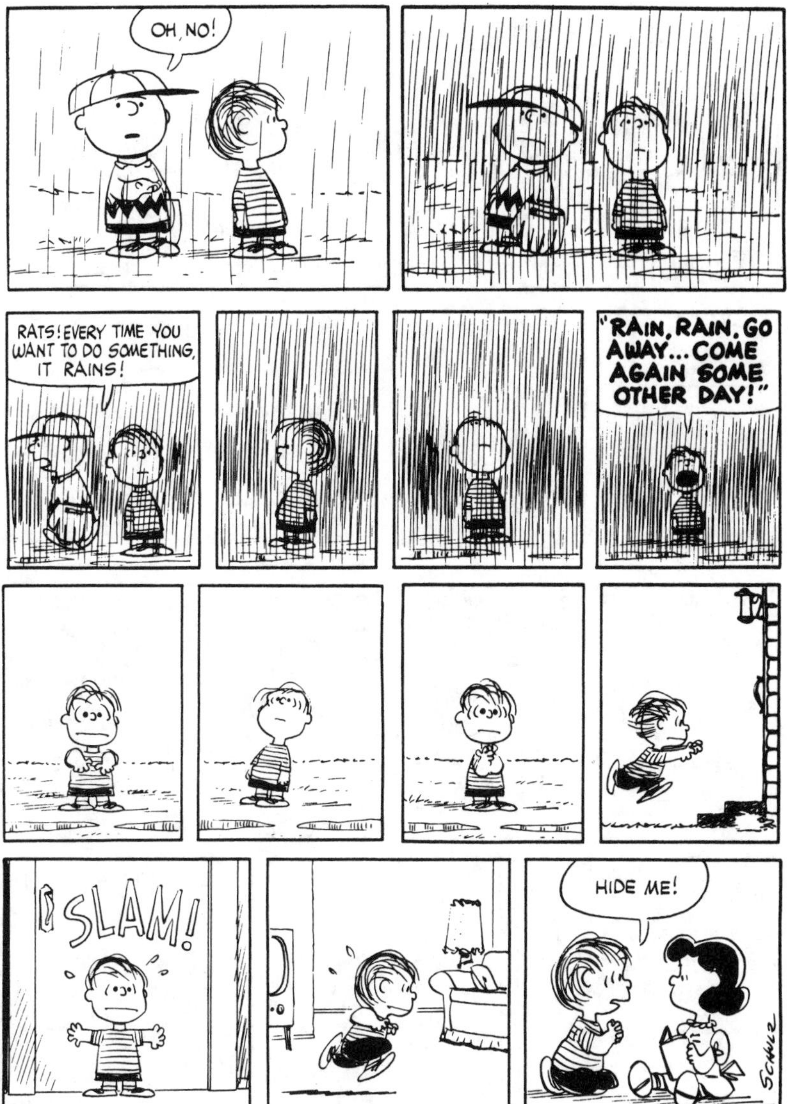

OH, NO!
RATS! EVERY TIME YOU WANT TO DO SOMETHING, IT RAINS!
"RAIN, RAIN, GO AWAY... COME AGAIN SOME OTHER DAY!"
SLAM!
HIDE ME!
SCHULZ

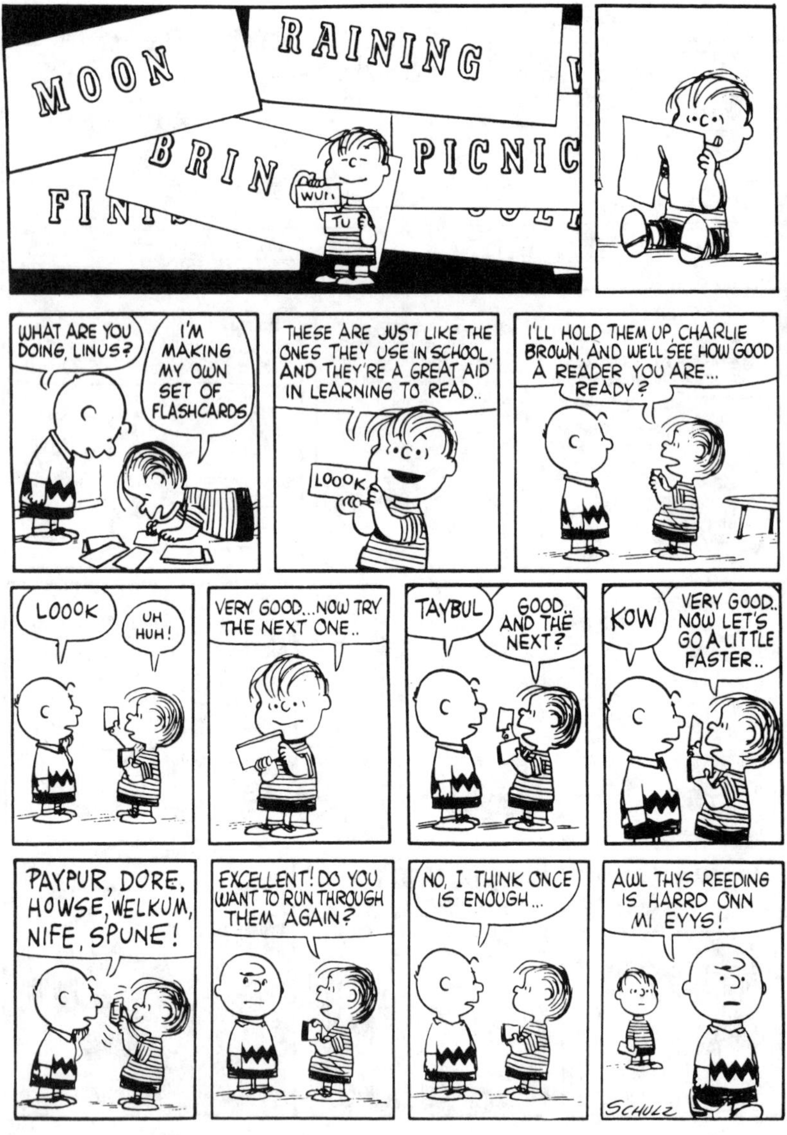
MOON
RAINING
BRIN
PICNIC
FIN
WUN
TU
WHAT ARE YOU DOING, LINUS?
I'M MAKING MY OWN SET OF FLASHCARDS
THESE ARE JUST LIKE THE ONES THEY USE IN SCHOOL, AND THEY'RE A GREAT AID IN LEARNING TO READ..
LOOOK
I'LL HOLD THEM UP, CHARLIE BROWN, AND WE'LL SEE HOW GOOD A READER YOU ARE... READY?
LOOOK
UH HUH!
VERY GOOD... NOW TRY THE NEXT ONE..
TAYBUL
GOOD.. AND THE NEXT?
KOW
VERY GOOD.. NOW LET'S GO A LITTLE FASTER..
PAYPUR, DORE, HOWSE, WELKUM, NIFE, SPUNE!
EXCELLENT! DO YOU WANT TO RUN THROUGH THEM AGAIN?
NO, I THINK ONCE IS ENOUGH...
AWL THYS REEDING IS HARRD ONN MI EYYS!
SCHULZ

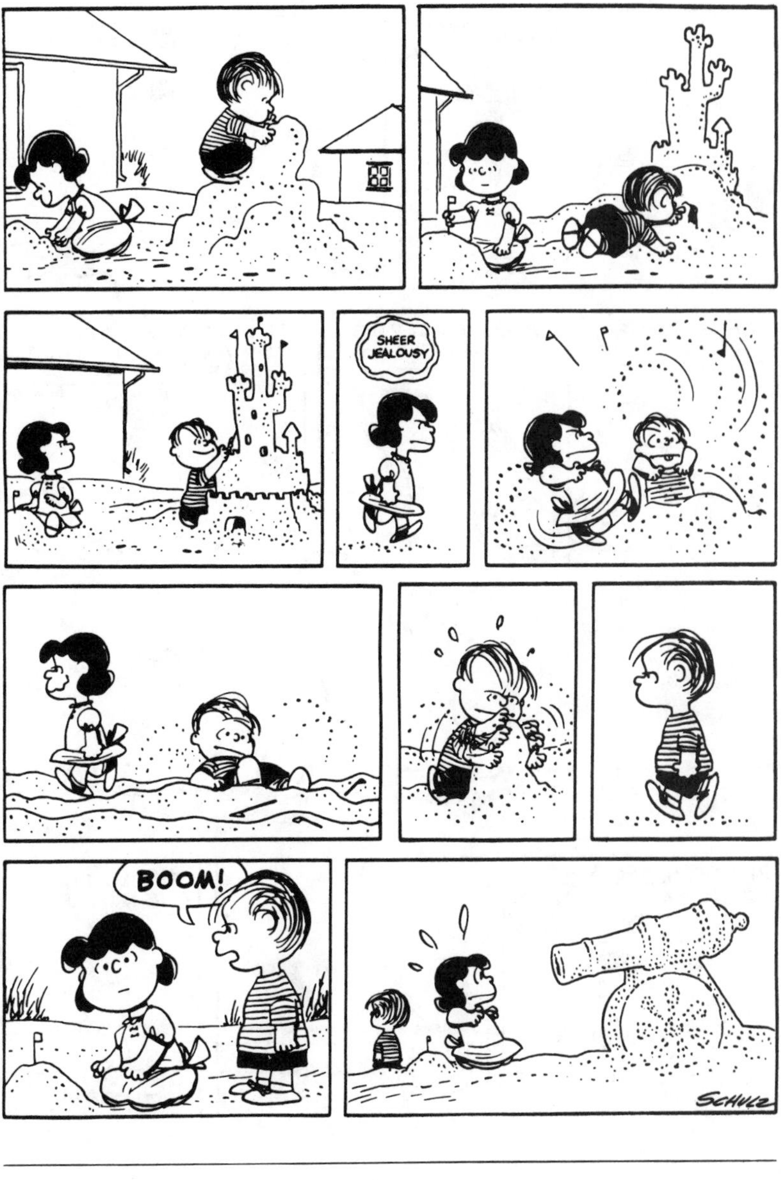
SHEER JEALOUSY
BOOM!
SCHULZ

SCHULZ
BUT IS IT ART?

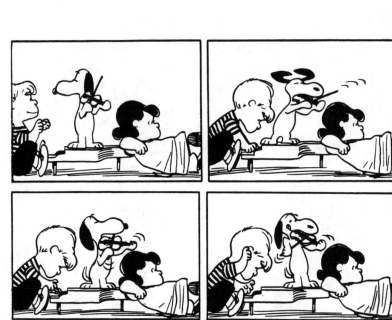

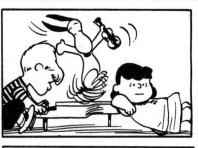

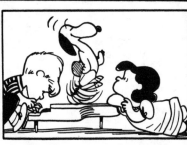

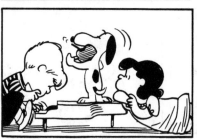

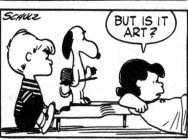

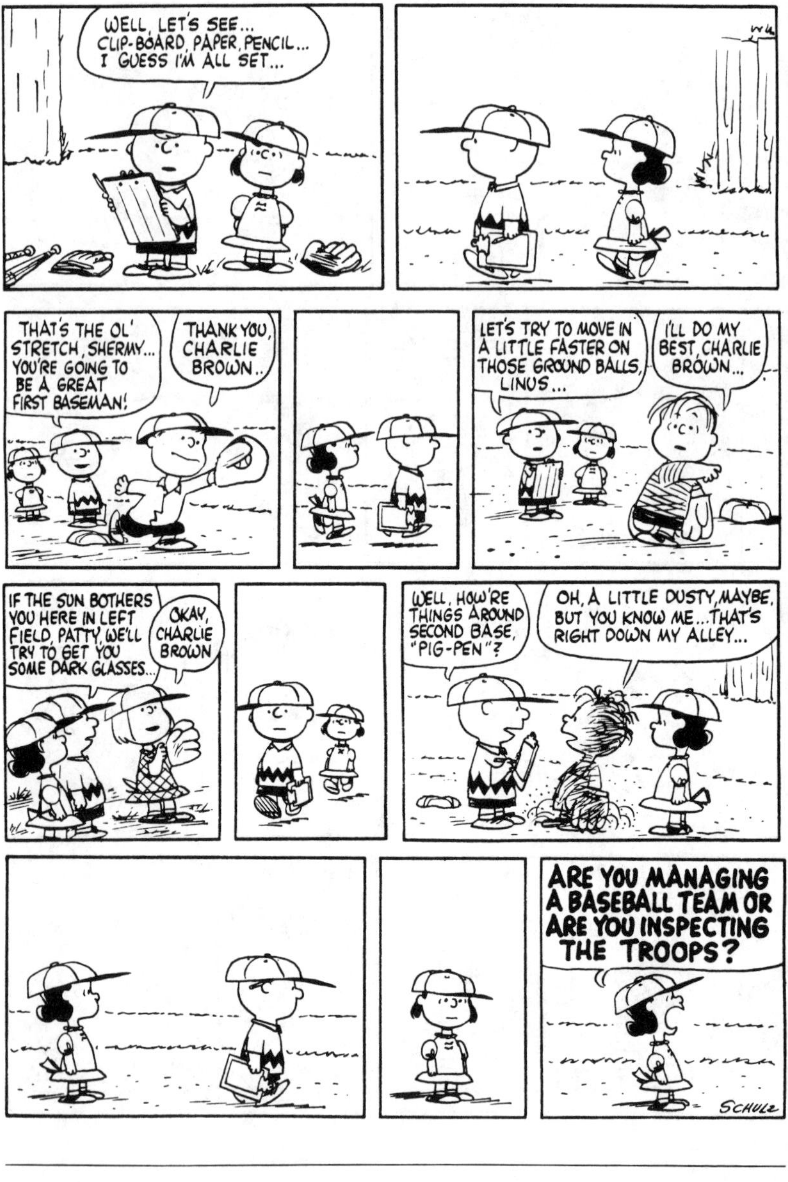
WELL, LET'S SEE... CLIP-BOARD, PAPER, PENCIL... I GUESS I'M ALL SET...
THAT'S THE OL' STRETCH, SHERMY... YOU'RE GOING TO BE A GREAT FIRST BASEMAN!
THANK YOU, CHARLIE BROWN..
LET'S TRY TO MOVE IN A LITTLE FASTER ON THOSE GROUND BALLS, LINUS...
I'LL DO MY BEST, CHARLIE BROWN...
IF THE SUN BOTHERS YOU HERE IN LEFT FIELD, PATTY, WE'LL TRY TO GET YOU SOME DARK GLASSES...
OKAY, CHARLIE BROWN
WELL, HOW'RE THINGS AROUND SECOND BASE, "PIG-PEN"?
OH, A LITTLE DUSTY, MAYBE, BUT YOU KNOW ME...THAT'S RIGHT DOWN MY ALLEY...
ARE YOU MANAGING A BASEBALL TEAM OR ARE YOU INSPECTING THE TROOPS?
SCHULZ

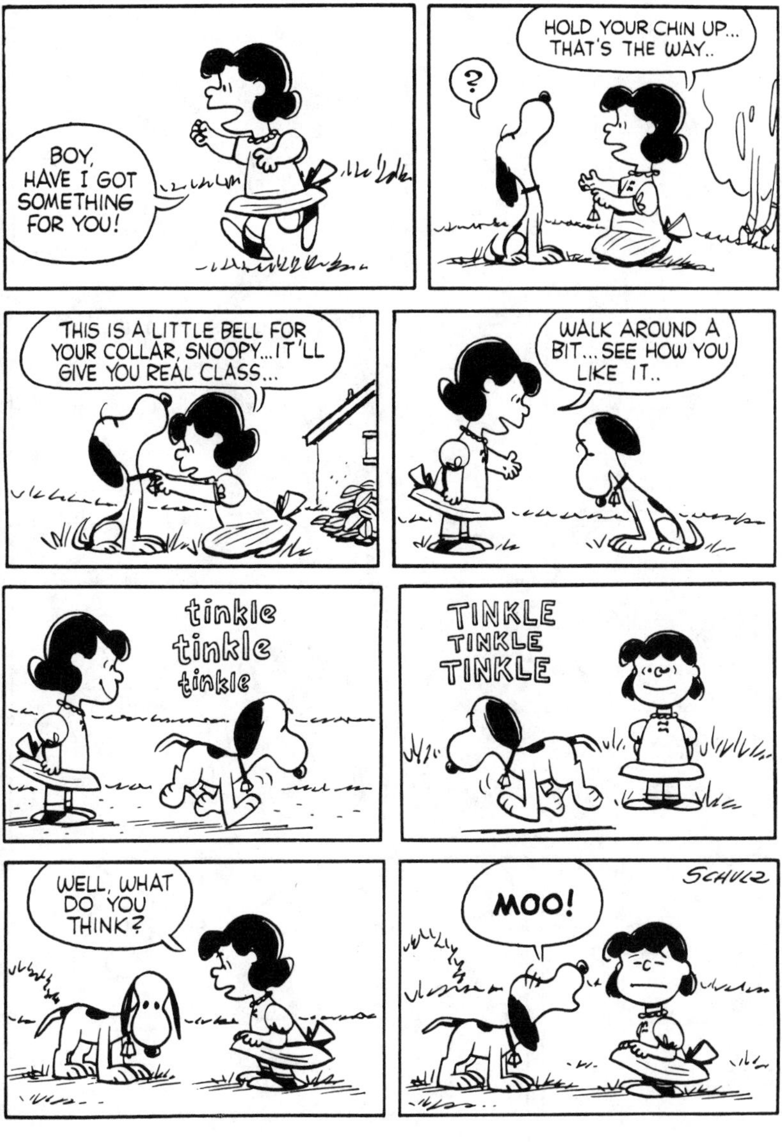
BOY, HAVE I GOT SOMETHING FOR YOU!
HOLD YOUR CHIN UP... THAT'S THE WAY..
?
THIS IS A LITTLE BELL FOR YOUR COLLAR, SNOOPY...IT'LL GIVE YOU REAL CLASS...
WALK AROUND A BIT...SEE HOW YOU LIKE IT..
tinkle tinkle tinkle
TINKLE TINKLE TINKLE
WELL, WHAT DO YOU THINK?
SCHULZ
MOO!

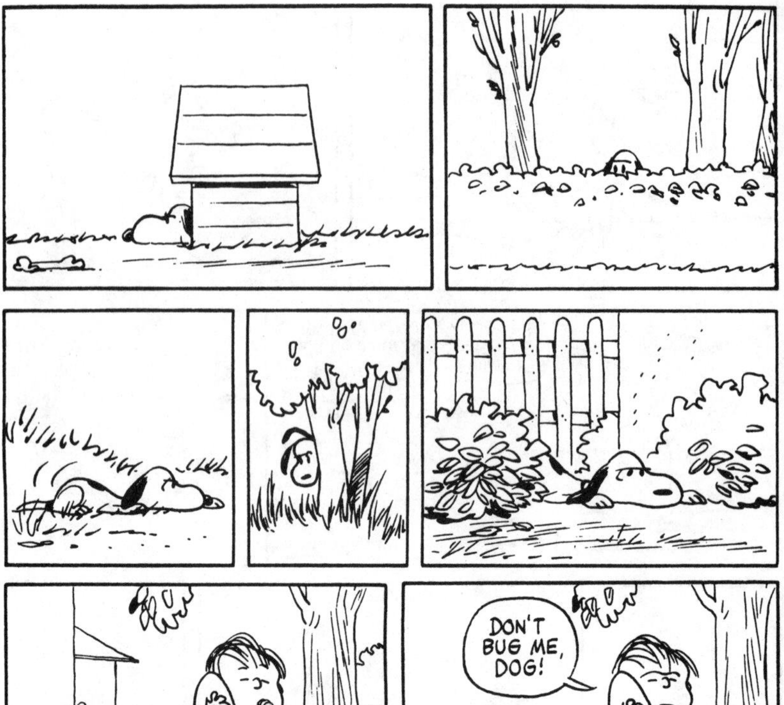
DON'T BUG ME, DOG!
* SIGH *
SCHULZ

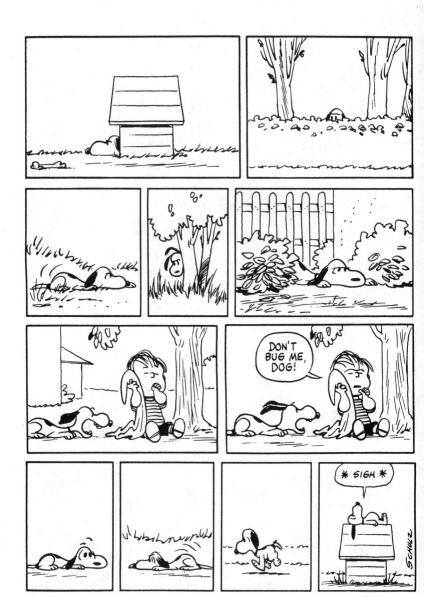

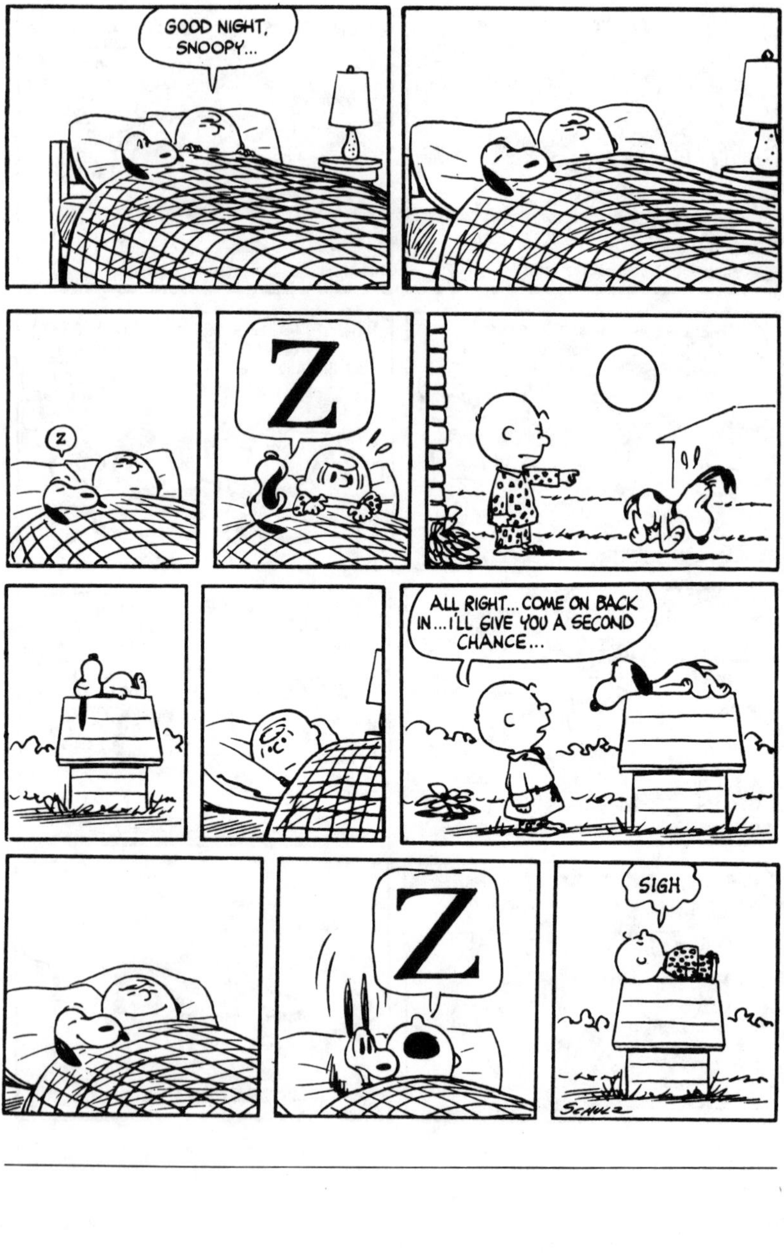
GOOD NIGHT, SNOOPY...
Z
Z
ALL RIGHT... COME ON BACK IN... I'LL GIVE YOU A SECOND CHANCE...
Z
SIGH
SCHULZ

WORLD'S NUMBER 1 FUSSBUDGET

CHAMP

STATE CHAMP

NATIONAL CHAMPION

WOR NUMB FUS

GIMME THAT BOOK! THAT'S **MY** BOOK!!

I DON'T WANNA WATCH THAT PROGRAM.. I WANNA WATCH **MY** PROGRAM!

ALL RIGHT, I'LL GO UPSTAIRS, AND LISTEN TO THE RADIO..

I DON'T WANNA LISTEN TO THAT PROGRAM... I WANNA LISTEN TO **MY** PROGRAM!!

ALL RIGHT... I'LL GO IN THE NEXT ROOM, AND PLAY A FEW RECORDS...

I DON'T WANNA LISTEN TO THOSE RECORDS.. I WANNA LISTEN TO MY RECORDS!

ALL RIGHT, I'LL GO OUTSIDE, AND LOOK AT THE STARS FOR A WHILE..

SCHULZ

I DON'T WANNA LOOK AT THOSE STARS..I WANNA LOOK AT MY...

*SIGH*

SCHROEDER, IF I TOLD YOU THAT I HAD THE FEELING YOU AND I WOULD GET MARRIED SOMEDAY, WOULD YOU CHUCKLE LIGHTLY OR LAUGH LOUD AND LONG?

I DON'T KNOW...IT'S KIND OF HARD TO SAY OFFHAND...

SCHROEDER, I HAVE THE FEELING THAT YOU AND I WILL GET MARRIED SOMEDAY...

HA HA HA HA HA HA

HO HO HO HO HA HA HA HA

HE'D LAUGH LOUD AND LONG!

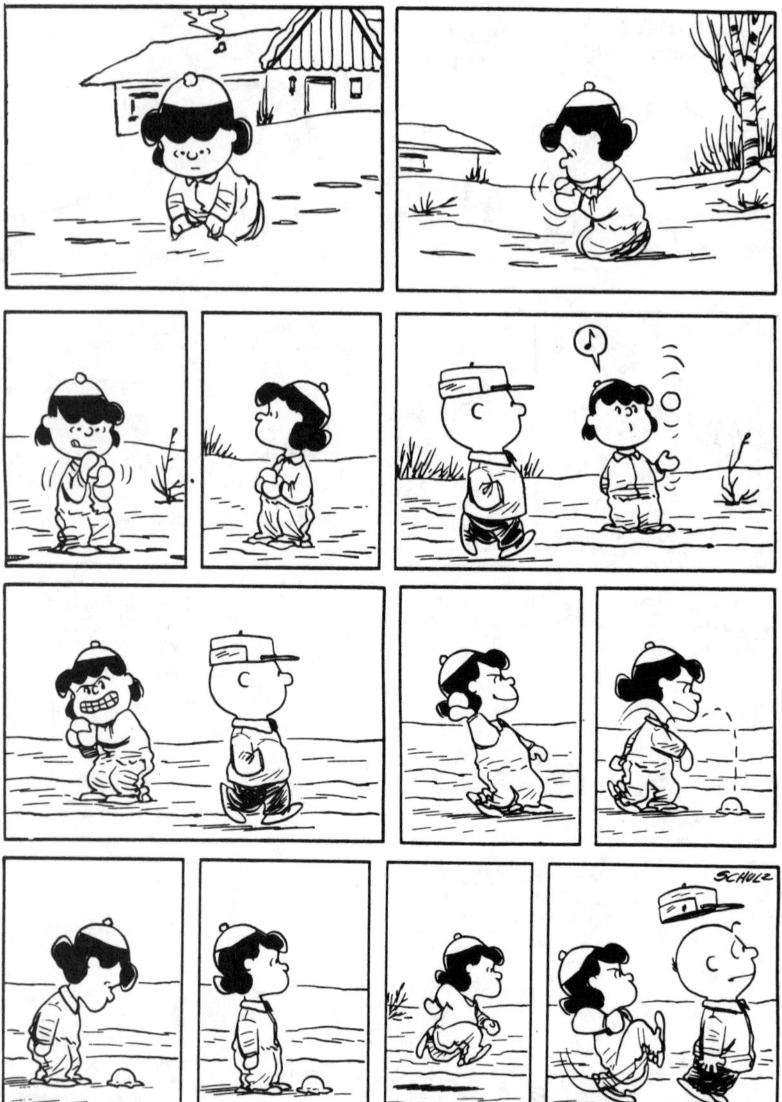
SCHULZ

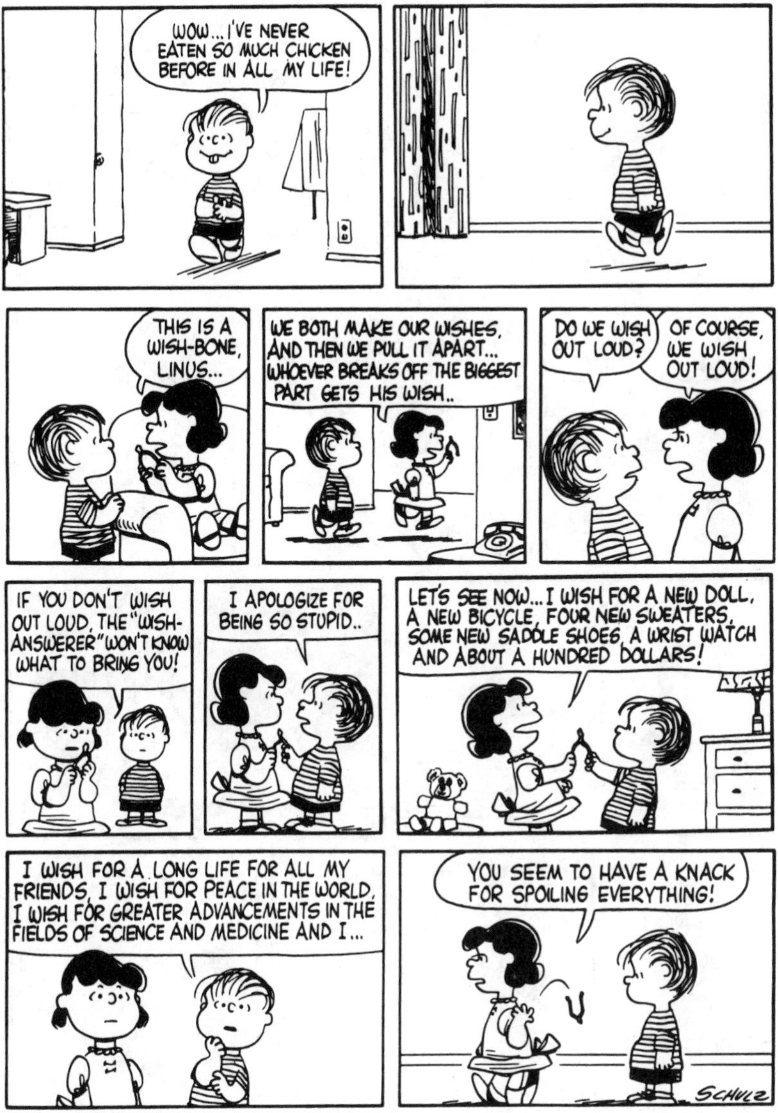
WOW...I'VE NEVER EATEN SO MUCH CHICKEN BEFORE IN ALL MY LIFE!
THIS IS A WISH-BONE, LINUS...
WE BOTH MAKE OUR WISHES, AND THEN WE PULL IT APART... WHOEVER BREAKS OFF THE BIGGEST PART GETS HIS WISH..
DO WE WISH OUT LOUD?
OF COURSE, WE WISH OUT LOUD!
IF YOU DON'T WISH OUT LOUD, THE "WISH-ANSWERER" WON'T KNOW WHAT TO BRING YOU!
I APOLOGIZE FOR BEING SO STUPID..
LET'S SEE NOW...I WISH FOR A NEW DOLL, A NEW BICYCLE, FOUR NEW SWEATERS, SOME NEW SADDLE SHOES, A WRIST WATCH AND ABOUT A HUNDRED DOLLARS!
I WISH FOR A LONG LIFE FOR ALL MY FRIENDS, I WISH FOR PEACE IN THE WORLD, I WISH FOR GREATER ADVANCEMENTS IN THE FIELDS OF SCIENCE AND MEDICINE AND I...
YOU SEEM TO HAVE A KNACK FOR SPOILING EVERYTHING!
SCHULZ

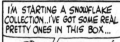

THERE'S A LESSON TO BE LEARNED HERE SOMEWHERE, BUT I DON'T KNOW WHAT IT IS...

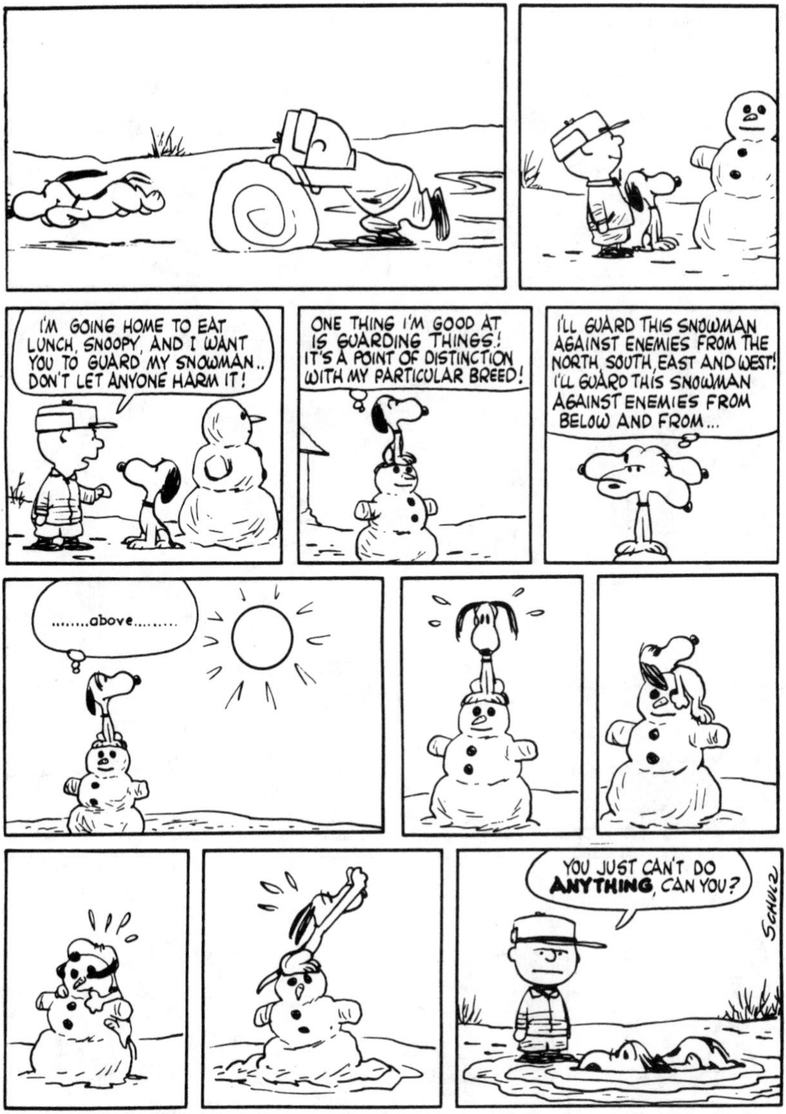
I'M GOING HOME TO EAT LUNCH, SNOOPY, AND I WANT YOU TO GUARD MY SNOWMAN.. DON'T LET ANYONE HARM IT!
ONE THING I'M GOOD AT IS GUARDING THINGS! IT'S A POINT OF DISTINCTION WITH MY PARTICULAR BREED!
I'LL GUARD THIS SNOWMAN AGAINST ENEMIES FROM THE NORTH, SOUTH, EAST AND WEST! I'LL GUARD THIS SNOWMAN AGAINST ENEMIES FROM BELOW AND FROM...
........above..........
YOU JUST CAN'T DO **ANYTHING**, CAN YOU?
SCHULZ

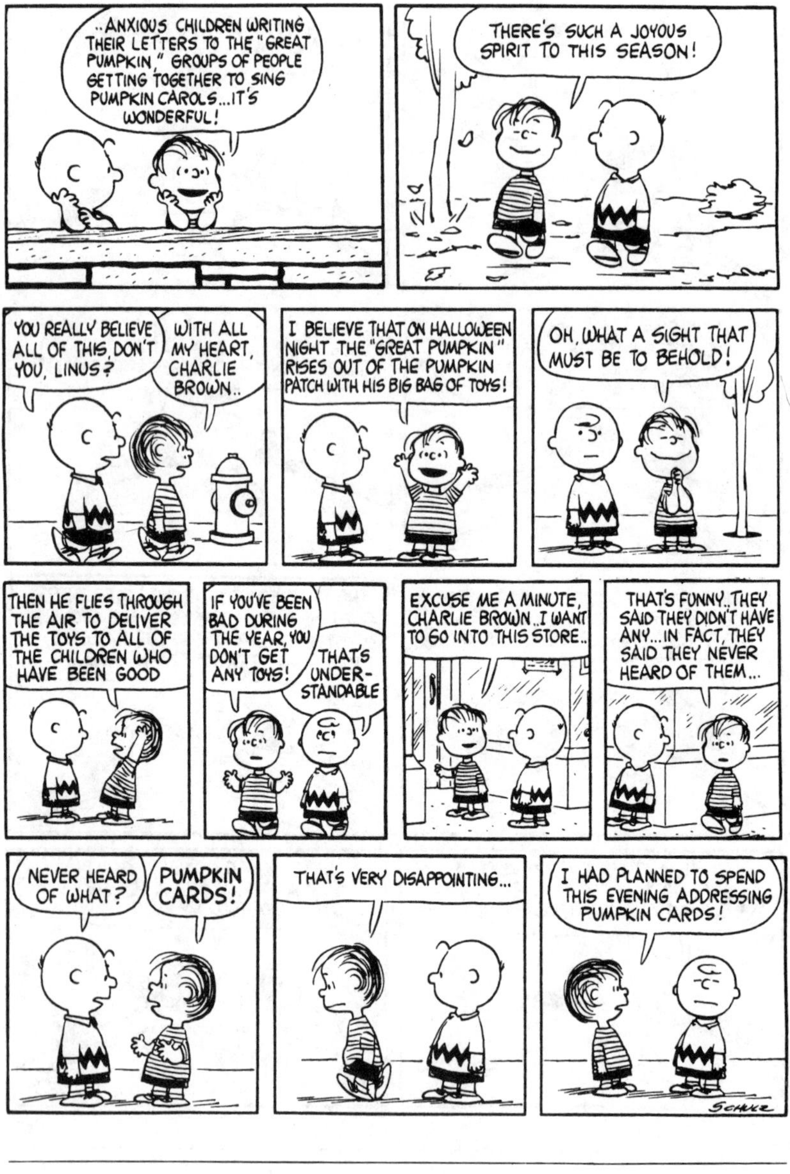
..ANXIOUS CHILDREN WRITING THEIR LETTERS TO THE "GREAT PUMPKIN," GROUPS OF PEOPLE GETTING TOGETHER TO SING PUMPKIN CAROLS...IT'S WONDERFUL!
THERE'S SUCH A JOYOUS SPIRIT TO THIS SEASON!
YOU REALLY BELIEVE ALL OF THIS, DON'T YOU, LINUS?
WITH ALL MY HEART, CHARLIE BROWN..
I BELIEVE THAT ON HALLOWEEN NIGHT THE "GREAT PUMPKIN" RISES OUT OF THE PUMPKIN PATCH WITH HIS BIG BAG OF TOYS!
OH, WHAT A SIGHT THAT MUST BE TO BEHOLD!
THEN HE FLIES THROUGH THE AIR TO DELIVER THE TOYS TO ALL OF THE CHILDREN WHO HAVE BEEN GOOD
IF YOU'VE BEEN BAD DURING THE YEAR, YOU DON'T GET ANY TOYS!
THAT'S UNDER-STANDABLE
EXCUSE ME A MINUTE, CHARLIE BROWN..I WANT TO GO INTO THIS STORE..
THAT'S FUNNY..THEY SAID THEY DIDN'T HAVE ANY...IN FACT, THEY SAID THEY NEVER HEARD OF THEM...
NEVER HEARD OF WHAT?
PUMPKIN CARDS!
THAT'S VERY DISAPPOINTING...
I HAD PLANNED TO SPEND THIS EVENING ADDRESSING PUMPKIN CARDS!
SCHULZ

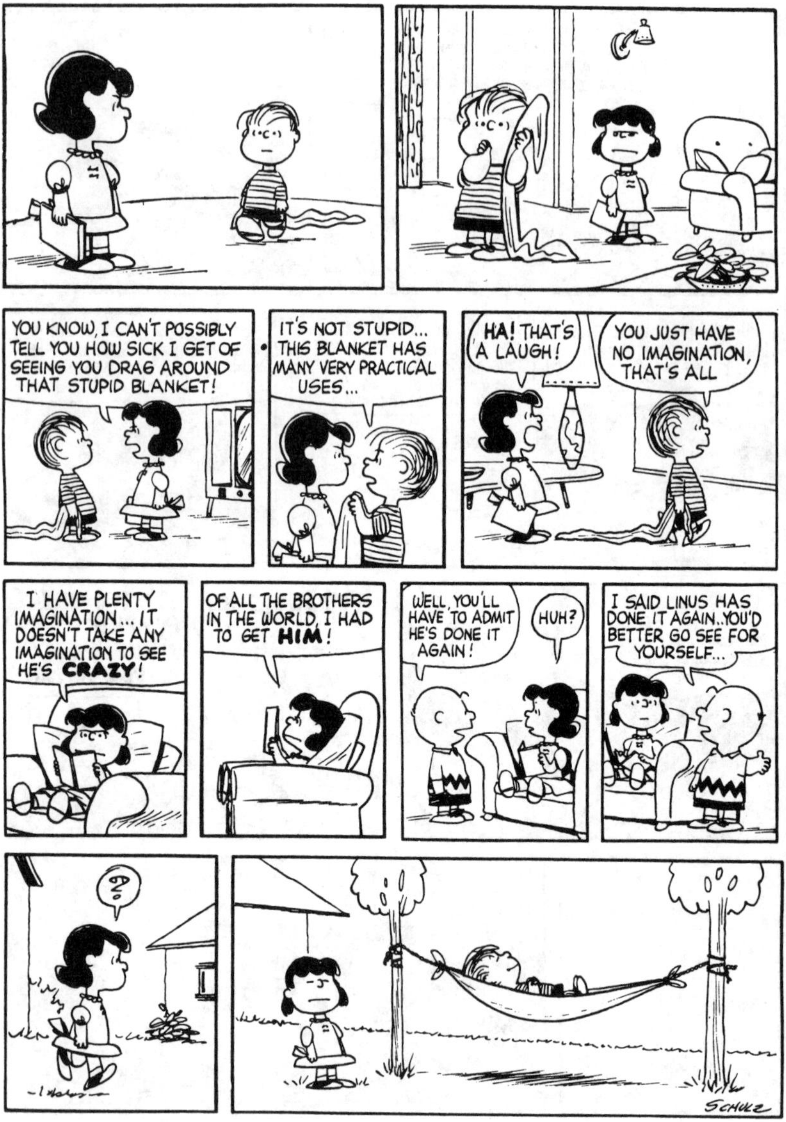
YOU KNOW, I CAN'T POSSIBLY TELL YOU HOW SICK I GET OF SEEING YOU DRAG AROUND THAT STUPID BLANKET!
IT'S NOT STUPID... THIS BLANKET HAS MANY VERY PRACTICAL USES...
HA! THAT'S A LAUGH!
YOU JUST HAVE NO IMAGINATION, THAT'S ALL
I HAVE PLENTY IMAGINATION... IT DOESN'T TAKE ANY IMAGINATION TO SEE HE'S CRAZY!
OF ALL THE BROTHERS IN THE WORLD, I HAD TO GET HIM!
WELL, YOU'LL HAVE TO ADMIT HE'S DONE IT AGAIN!
HUH?
I SAID LINUS HAS DONE IT AGAIN..YOU'D BETTER GO SEE FOR YOURSELF...
?
SCHULZ

SCHULZ

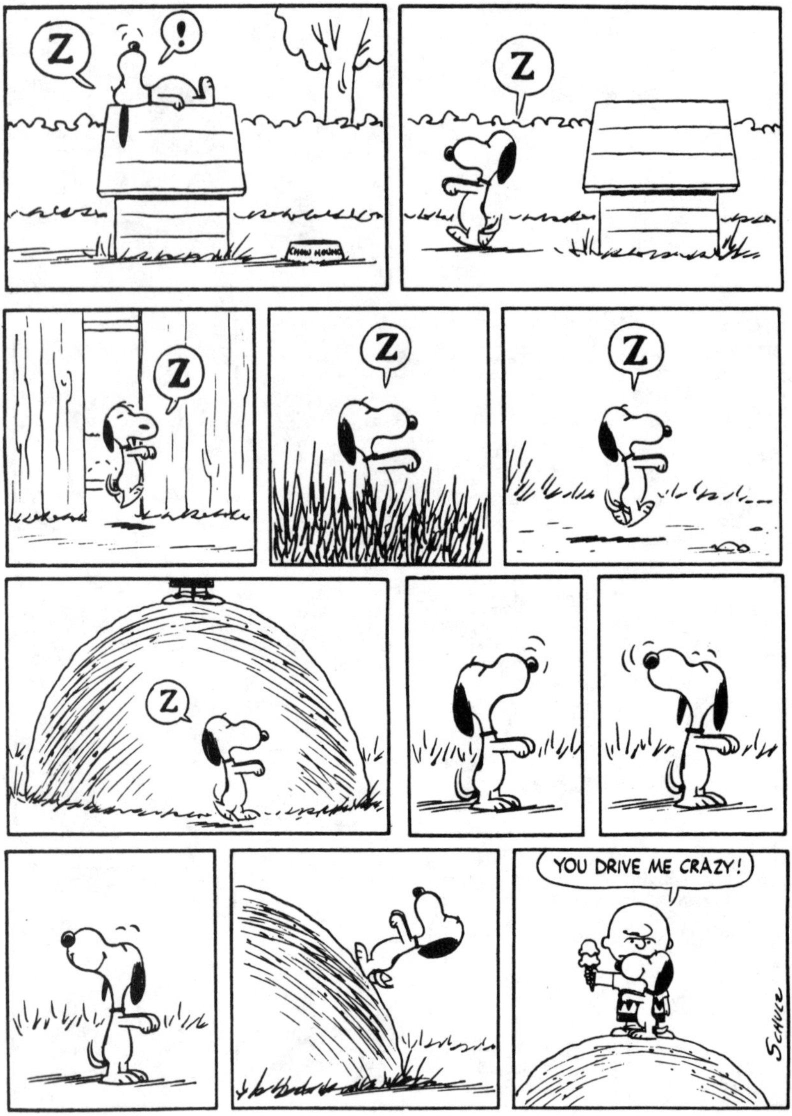
Z
!
CHOW HOUND
Z
Z
Z
Z
Z
YOU DRIVE ME CRAZY!
SCHULZ